THE HOUND OF
THE SANIBEL SUNSET
DETECTIVE

Also by Ron Base

Fiction

Matinee Idol
Foreign Object
Splendido
Magic Man
The Strange
The Sanibel Sunset Detective
The Sanibel Sunset Detective Returns
Another Sanibel Sunset Detective
The Two Sanibel Sunset Detectives

Non-fiction

The Movies of the Eighties (with David Haslam)
If the Other Guy Isn't Jack Nicholson, I've Got the Part
Marquee Guide to Movies on Video
Cuba Portrait of an Island (with Donald Nausbaum)

www.ronbase.com
Read Ron's blog at
www.ronbase.wordpress.com
Contact Ron at
ronbase@ronbase.com

THE HOUND OF THE SANIBEL SUNSET DETECTIVE

a novel

RON BASE

Copyright, the Canadian Copyright Licensing Agency,
One Yonge Street, Toronto, Ontario, M6B 3A9.
Library and Archives Canada Cataloguing in Publication
Base, Ron, 1948-, author
        The hound of the Sanibel sunset detective / Ron Base.
    ISBN 978-0-9736955-8-8 (pbk.)
    I. Title.
    PS8553.A784H68 2014   C813'.54   C2014-906530-2

West-End Books
133 Mill St.
Milton, Ontario
L9T 1S1

Cover design: Ann Kornuta
Text design: Ric Base
Electronic formatting: Ric Base
Sanibel-Captiva map: Ann Kornuta

FIRST EDITION

For Clinton and Marley

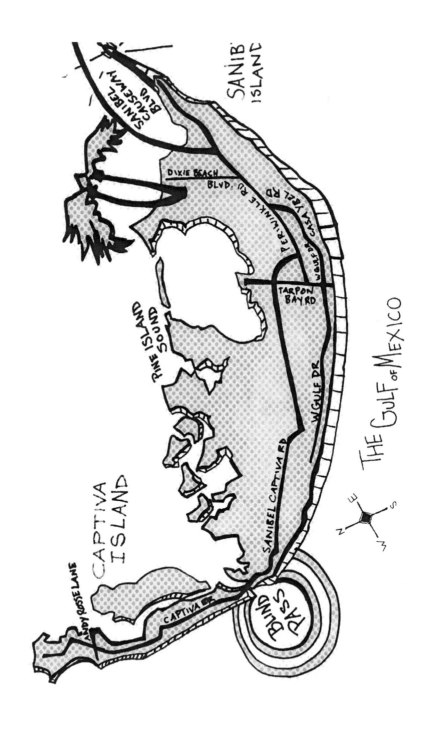

ART WORTH TWO MILLION DOLLARS STOLEN FROM MUSEUM

MONTREAL (CP)—Thieves broke into the Montreal Museum of Fine Art over the Labor Day weekend and made off with jewelry and Rembrandt's *Landscape with Cottages*.

According to police, three men, armed with sawed-off shotguns, employing the same equipment used to scale telephone poles, climbed a tree adjacent to the museum shortly after midnight Saturday in order to gain access to the two-story 1912 Beaux-Arts building through a skylight that was under repair.

A plastic sheet placed over the skylight had neutralized the security alarm. The trio opened the skylight and slid down a 15-meter nylon cord to the second floor, police say.

At 1.30 a.m., one intruder twice fired a 12-pump shotgun into the ceiling when a guard completing his rounds hesitated before dropping to the floor.

Two other guards were overpowered, bound, and gagged. All three guards were then held at gunpoint by one of their assailants.

After spending 30 minutes selecting paintings and jewelry, the thieves used a guard's key to open the door of the museum's panel truck parked in the garage. In the process, a side door alarm was tripped and the trio escaped on foot, abandoning 15 paintings by artists such as El Greco, Picasso, and Tintoretto, but stealing 39 pieces of jewelry.

They also got away with *Landscape with Cottages*, painted by the Dutch master Rembrandt Harmenszoon van Rijn in 1654 and valued at one million dollars.

—*Canadian Press* news story, September 5, 1972

1

"So you really are leaving," Rex Baxter said.

"I'm not leaving, I'm retiring," Tree Callister said.

"It comes down to the same thing," Rex said. He did not sound happy. He and Tree had been friends since Tree was a young reporter in Chicago, and Rex, a former B-movie actor in Hollywood, hosted an afternoon cable TV movie show. This was long before Rex became president of the Sanibel-Captiva Chamber of Commerce and Tree, retired from the newspaper business, appointed himself Sanibel Island's only private detective.

Rex, ageless and forever dapper an old lion in his comfortable, sun-drenched winter—had returned from a two-week visit to the Windy City in time to witness Tree packing up the office Rex had "rented" to him at the Chamber of Commerce Visitors Center located just over the causeway on Sanibel Island. Rent was a rather loosely applied term, since Rex never actually collected it.

"Don't even think about taking that Scotch tape dispenser," Rex said as he watched Tree lift it off the shelf behind the office desk.

"Is it yours?" Tree said.

"It's not mine," Rex corrected. "It is the property of the Sanibel-Captiva Chamber of Commerce.

"Then I had better not take it," Tree said.

He placed the dispenser back on the shelf and looked dolefully at the nearly empty box open on the desk.

"Not much to show for your life as a private detective," Rex observed.

"I carry a lot of memories out into the world," Tree said.

"Fond memories of all those people who shot you," Rex said.

"Only two people shot me," Tree said.

"Let's face it, Tree. Most people get through an entire lifetime without being shot at all."

Irrefutable logic there.

Everyone on Sanibel Island had thought Tree crazy to become a private detective in the first place. Even his wife, Freddie, who had stuck by him after he was downsized from the *Chicago Sun-Times,* the newspaper where he had worked for most of his adult life, wondered at his sanity. Maybe it was getting shot that second time, maybe that was the straw that broke the camel's back—or the shot that killed the camel. Or something. But now Tree figured enough was enough, and he had decided he was not cut out for the life of a private eye so it was time to give up The Sanibel Sunset Detective Agency. Not that there was much to give up.

"You can put that electric pencil sharpener back while you're at it," Rex said.

"I was sure that was my pencil sharpener."

"Strictly on loan from the Chamber of Commerce."

Tree returned the pencil sharpener to its spot beside the tape dispenser.

"I don't know why I bothered to bring in this box," Tree said.

"I don't know why you're doing this," Rex said.

"You said it yourself. People keep shooting me."

"I think it has a lot more to do with Freddie," Rex said.

"There's no doubt about it," Tree said. "Freddie prefers a husband who is alive."

"Come on outside," Rex said.

"What? You're going to beat me up because I tried to steal your pencil sharpener?"

"There's something I want to show you," Rex said.

A fire-engine red car, shimmering under the morning sun, was parked in the area reserved for Chamber employees. Rex led Tree over to it.

"How do you like it?" he asked Tree.

"You're kidding. Is this yours?"

"The new Dodge Challenger Hellcat."

"You're driving a red car nicknamed the Hellcat?"

"Seeing as how I'm something of a hellcat myself," Rex said.

"That's certainly how I've always described you," Tree said.

"Seven hundred horsepower. Six hundred and fifty pound-feet of torque."

"What's that mean?"

"It means the car goes like a bat out of hell," Rex said.

"Just what you need on Sanibel," Tree offered.

He leaned down and peered into the car. "With that dashboard, you could land on the moon."

"Super-charged Hemi V-8 engine," Rex said.

"I have no idea what that means," Tree said.

"I met someone in Chicago," Rex said.

That stopped Tree. "What's that got to do with a Hemi V-8?"

"It doesn't have anything to do with it. That's what they call a segue, in case you didn't know."

"It's a lousy segue," Tree said. "Besides which, I don't understand. You're Rex Baxter. You meet people all the time. You can't walk down the street without meeting someone."

"No, no," Rex said. "I *met* someone. As in I met someone."

"You mean a member of the opposite sex."

"Yes, that's what I mean," Rex said. "Boy, sometimes you are pretty damn slow on the uptake. Maybe you really shouldn't be a detective."

"That's been suggested any number of times," Tree said.

"She's coming here," Rex said.

"You mean this member of the opposite sex you met in Chicago?"

"Correct," Rex said.

"She's coming here."

"Let me know which parts of this you're having trouble with, and I will gladly repeat them slowly for you," Rex said.

"That's great," Tree said. "She'll like the Hellcat."

"I didn't get the car because of her," Rex insisted.

"It's high time you met someone," Tree said. "When's she coming?"

"Tomorrow," Rex said.

"That was quick," Tree said.

Rex looked at Tree uneasily and then shrugged. "I've been alone too long. It's time I did something about it."

"I'm glad for you, Rex," Tree said.

"Besides, you're deserting me."

"All I'm doing is moving out of the office. Except, it turns out, there's nothing to move."

"I saw you put a pen in your pocket," Rex said. "That's Chamber property, too."

Tree sighed and gave him back the pen.

———

Tree arrived home to an empty house on Andy Rosse Lane. Freddie would not return for hours. She was busy running five Florida supermarkets, including Dayton's on Sanibel Island, that she recently had acquired. Well, to be accurate, Freddie herself had not purchased the stores, but she had put together the syndicate of investors that had, and now oversaw day-to-day store operations, a job that kept her away from home a lot more than Tree would have liked, but also a job that was making her, and by extension, him, rich.

It was certainly a job that did not need the distractions that came with the Sanibel Sunset Detective Agency, distractions that to the surprise of both of them, had left Freddie concerned that her husband would not live long enough or stay out of jail long enough to enjoy the financial fruits of her endeavors.

Well, now he would live, Tree mused as he thumped around the empty house, wondering what to do for lunch. He was no longer the Sanibel Sunset Detective. He was plain W. Tremain Callister, former Chicago newspaperman, a retiree living on Sanibel-Captiva just like so many others. Who was he, then? And what was his purpose in life? His purpose, he reckoned, was not to get himself killed, and to make Freddie happy. That should keep him busy.

Shouldn't it?

He thought about phoning Rex to see if he wanted to have lunch, but decided against it seeing as how he had just come from the Visitors Center, and if he phoned Rex this soon, Rex would correctly divine that Tree, having just vacated the detective business an hour earlier, had no earthly idea what to do with himself.

Instead, he left the house and wandered down Andy Rosse Lane toward the beach to the Mucky Duck restaurant hoping to find a table outside and order a sandwich. But the Mucky Duck was full of lunching tourists with a lineup outside waiting to get in. He walked a few yards farther to the beach, marveling yet again at how many people of all ages and skin colors baked under a hot noonday sun, unafraid of the looming horrors of skin cancer—unlike himself, the pasty Chicago guy who feared the sun would melt him.

Tree made his way back along the street choked with noonday crowds checking out the various shops, trying to get into the restaurants. He wondered yet again if he and Freddie had known about all the traffic, whether or not they would have bought a house on the street.

His cellphone in the pocket of his cargo shorts awakened with an electronic buzz. He awkwardly fished it out and tried to swipe it open. Only it wouldn't open. Damn! The smartphone continually outsmarted him. After the third try, he finally got it open, punched the green icon, and heard Edith Goldman say, "Tree? Is that you?"

"It's me, Edith," Tree said. Edith was Tree's lawyer from nearby Fort Myers. She had the habit of looking him up and down as though measuring him for an orange jumpsuit. Maybe it was because she had had to bail him out of jail more times than he liked to think about.

"I've been phoning your office, trying to get hold of you."

"I'm not there," Tree said.

"I know you're not there. Where are you?"

"I'm retired," he said.

"You're what?" As though she had not heard right.

"I've closed the agency. I'm retiring. I thought I told you."

"You never said a word." Edith sounded irritated by this news. "What are you doing retiring?"

"No one should know better than you why I'm quitting," Tree said. "Considering the number of times you've had to get me out of jail, I thought you'd be pleased."

She did not sound at all pleased. "You can't retire. Not yet, anyway."

"Why not?"

"Because I need you to do something for me. I need you to do it quickly, and I need you not to ask too many questions."

"Like I said, Edith, I've closed the office. I'm out of it."

"Be out of it tomorrow," Edith said curtly. "Today I want you to drive to Miami and speak to a client."

"Edith, I can't do that."

"I'll pay you one thousand dollars, Tree. My client needs a private detective and you're the only one I could come up with on short notice."

"Thanks a lot," Tree said.

"All you have to do is speak to this guy."

"What guy?"

"He's Canadian. A client from Montreal. An older gentleman. I've represented him for a number of years now. He wants to hire a private detective, and I recommended you. Just drive down there this afternoon and talk to him. Then everybody's happy."

"Edith, Freddie's going to kill me."

"If there's any problem, I'll remind Freddie of the number of times I bailed you out of trouble. Besides, I've already said you'd meet him this afternoon. Do this for me. Please."

Tree exhaled loudly as he reached the front of his house. "What's the address?"

"Thank you, Tree." Edith sounded relieved. "My client's name is Vic Trinchera. He's a Montreal businessman who retired to Miami a few years ago. Do you know where the Biltmore Hotel is in Coral Gables?"

"Vaguely," Tree said.

"He lives down the street from the hotel. He's expecting you around two o'clock."

"What did you tell him about me?"

"What do you think I told him? I told him you were the best private detective in Florida."

"Edith, I am not the best private detective in Florida," Tree said.

"I know that, and you know that," Edith said. "But for the moment, let's not tell Vic."

2

As his battered Volkswagen Beetle convertible rumbled and clattered along I-75, the ribbon of four-lane asphalt known as Alligator Alley bisecting the flat swath of the Florida Everglades, Tree tried calling Freddie on his smartphone.

"I can barely hear you," Tree said.

"I asked how you're enjoying your retirement so far." Freddie's voice broke up in a rain of static.

"You're not going to like this," he said.

"What?"

"I'm crossing Alligator Alley. Headed for Miami."

"There's something wrong with this connection. I thought you said something about Alligator Alley."

"I'm driving to Miami." Tree was yelling into his phone.

Freddie said, "Why would you be going to Miami?"

"Edith Goldman called. She has a client she wants me to talk to."

"Did you say Edith? As in Goldman?"

"He needs a private detective. She suggested me."

"Except you are no longer a private detective."

"That's right," Tree agreed. "But Edith was insistent. He's a Canadian businessman, apparently. I'm just going to meet with him, that's all."

Freddie's voice rose over the static: "Tree, you've barely left your office, and already you're taking another assignment."

"I'm not taking an assignment. Like I say, I'm just going to talk to this guy—as a favor to Edith."

"A what?"

"A favor. A favor to Edith. At least that's what I'm telling myself."

"When do you think you'll be home?"

"As soon as I can."

"I'm losing you," Freddie said.

"I'll be back in time for dinner. How's that?"

"What?"

"Dinner. I will make it home for dinner." Enunciating each word carefully, as if that would somehow make a bad connection better.

"Please, please be careful," Freddie said.

"As I may have mentioned before, Careful is my middle name."

"No, Tree, it isn't," Freddie said.

———————

By the time Tree saw the imposing facade of the Biltmore—its distinctive minaret-style bell tower once made the hotel the tallest building in Florida—he had to go to the bathroom. Badly. The shortcomings of age; you could never be too far from a toilet.

Rather than hold on until he got to Vic Trinchera's place, he veered onto the drive leading to the Biltmore's front entrance. A sandy-haired eager-beaver wearing a dove-gray suit opened the driver's door for him, announcing, "Welcome to the Biltmore, sir. My name is Justin. I'm at your service. How are you, today?"

"I'm okay," Tree said, grimacing as he eased himself out, hip aching, sciatic nerve throbbing—more disillusioning signs of age.

"Well, sir, we're delighted to have you with us," Justin said with grave sincerity. "Did you know, sir, that the Biltmore was built in 1926?"

"I'm only going to be a few minutes," Tree said. "Is that okay?"

"That's fine, sir. I'm not certain you're aware of this, but Johnny Weismuller, the world-famous Tarzan of the movies, used to be a swimming instructor here."

"I didn't know that," Tree said.

"This was before he became Tarzan, of course. Did you know the pool where he taught is still here? It used to be the world's largest swimming pool."

"It isn't any more?" Tree said.

This momentarily confounded Justin. "Why, I'm not sure, sir. I guess someone built a larger pool somewhere. Are you checking in with us today?"

"I'm looking for the restroom," Tree said, loins aching.

"Directly through the lobby to your left, sir. Just let me know when you want the car, and I'll bring it around for you."

Finally shaking off Justin, Tree hobbled into the hotel. Despite the urgency of his mission, Tree could not help but pause before the stately magnificence of the Biltmore lobby: the moist lusciousness of the plants and ferns, the massive leather arm chairs, the vault ceilings supported by a straight line of thick marble columns, the sunlight streaming in through French doors lining the far wall that could not quite dispel musty pomp and circumstance.

He loved these great old Florida hotels—this one, the Breakers in Palm Beach, the Casa Marina in Key West—great dinosaurs from a bygone era of stately luxury that somehow survived, mostly intact, into the twenty-first century. Tree recalled reading tales of ghosts at the Biltmore. He could imagine they lingered in the dark corners of the lobby, perhaps waiting for Johnny Weismuller, Tarzan himself, to give them swimming lessons in what once had been the world's largest swimming pool.

But Johnny wasn't about to show up today, and Tree Callister really did have to get to the bathroom. He found the men's room off the lobby, went through the swinging door into its discreetly lit, marbled interior and pushed open one of the cubicles. He stood over the toilet, wondering about a life culminating in a ceaseless search, not for meaning, but for an available bathroom.

Outside his cubicle, the bathroom door opened and some- one stepped across the floor.

"No, I'm still at the Biltmore." The voice sounded raspy and hollow, echoing in the marble interior. "We're having something to eat. We were starving, that's why. We're going over there a little later. No hurry. It's not like he's into hitting the South Beach clubs at night. Most days, Vic don't even leave the house." There was a pause, and then, "Yeah, yeah, Johnny. Not to worry. We'll take care of it. It's done. You want the egg broken, we break the egg. That's what I do, that's my business, okay? I don't need advice on how to do my business."

The room went quiet. Tree stood frozen in place. Present- ly, there was the sound of a zipper coming down and then the splash into a urinal, accompanied by a sigh from the man with the raspy voice.

A moment later the urinal's automatic flushing unit went into action. Then there was the sound of water gushing into a sink. Shortly after that, Tree heard the entrance door swing open and hiss closed again.

You want the egg broken, we break the egg.

Did that mean what it sounded like it meant? Tree did him- self up and opened the cubicle door, moving over to the sink. He took his time washing and drying his hands before re-en- tering the lobby. Ahead, he could see a tall man in a loose white shirt sway through a set of glass-paneled doors. Tree went past a framed sepia photograph of the actor Gene Kelly wearing a cap at a jaunty angle, posing at the Cannes Film Festival.

Tree stepped through the glass doors and was confront- ed by a long, tiled concourse opening onto a pretty courtyard around a fountain. Wrought-iron tables and chairs lined the concourse. Tree watched as the man in the white shirt took an empty seat at a table occupied by two other men.

One of the men wore a straw hat shading a pasty, pock-marked face, a member perhaps of a jazz trio that got together to play dives on weekends. The other man was bare-headed, almost bald, someone's exhausted grandfather. The two men already at the table were drinking beer. The white-shirted man looked to be in his fifties with a puffy, tanned face, a thin mouth framed by a carefully trimmed mustache and goatee.

Tree went back through the door and then crossed the lobby and went out to where Justin stood waiting expectantly for the next guest he could illuminate with his pocket history of the Biltmore. He flashed another eager smile as Tree approached. "Boy, that didn't take long, sir."

"Justin, I need my car," Tree said.

"Leaving us so soon?"

"I'm leaving right now," Tree said.

"I'm so sorry to hear that."

"Justin, I need the car...*now*."

Tree glanced around, half expecting the three men from the courtyard to burst out the door to confront him: what was he doing peeing in the men's room? More to the point, why was he watching them? What was he up to? But no one came out the door. A few minutes later, the Beetle sputtered into view with Justin behind the wheel. He held the door open for Tree who handed him a ten-dollar bill. Justin frowned at it. "Come back and see us again soon, sir." He didn't sound enthusiastic about the prospect.

Apparently, ten dollars did not buy a lot of love at the Biltmore.

3

Maybe it was nothing. Maybe the guy with the goatee was talking about another Vic. But then maybe he wasn't. Maybe the guy had been talking on his cellphone in the bathroom about Tree's Vic—Vic Trinchera, Edith Goldman's client whom he was supposed to meet in a few minutes. If it was the same Vic Trinchera, then he might be in trouble. What the blazes had Edith gotten him mixed up in?

The streets of Coral Gables, neat and tidy—and empty—under the bright noontime sun, were flanked by handsome Spanish-style homes reflecting comfortable, tasteful prosperity in a lush tropical setting.

The Anastasia Avenue address Edith had given him was less than five minutes from the Biltmore. If those three were coming for Vic Trinchera, they would not have far to travel—which meant Tree didn't have a whole lot of time.

He brought the Beetle to a stop in front of a Mediterranean-style bungalow with a red tile roof. It was a pleasant home but less elegant than the neighbors' places, partially hidden behind a mixture of banyan and palm trees. Tree got out of the car, went to the door, and rang the bell.

When no one answered after a couple of moments, he rang again. The door opened and Tree found himself confronted by a tiny, gray man in a blue gym suit. The gray man's long, horse-like face was topped by a Greek fisherman's cap, pushed back on his forehead. He looked as though he was on his way to a bingo game at the Senior Citizen's Home.

He said, "Yeah?" as though annoyed at being interrupted en route to the big game.

"Mr. Trinchera?"

The small, dark eyes shaded by the peak of the fisherman's cap filled with suspicion. "Who's asking?" he demanded.

"Edith Goldman sent me," Tree said.

The suspicion in Trinchera's eyes dissolved somewhat. "You Callister?"

Tree nodded. "I'm Tree Callister."

"You're late," Trinchera snapped. "But come on in."

Tree stepped into a cool interior while Vic Trinchera carefully closed the door and turned to his visitor. "You strapped?"

"What?"

"Strapped? You carry a gun?"

"No," Tree said.

Trinchera looked surprised, and then skeptical. "I don't like guns in the house, you understand."

"I don't have a gun."

"Okay then, that's fine. Follow me."

They went into a darkened living room full of old furniture: a floral print sofa pushed against the wall, a couple of sickly green recliners aimed at a flatscreen television. A framed painting of a Florida bird hung above the sofa. Tree could not tell what kind of bird it was. The furniture looked scruffy and out of place, as though after the purchase of the lovely house in the elegant neighborhood, there was no money left for furniture.

"Sit down there, Callister." Vic Trinchera pointed a shaky finger in the direction of the sofa.

Tree seated himself. Trinchera said, "I haven't been well," as though to explain the shaky finger.

He slumped onto one of the recliners, abruptly looking tired. "This weather gets to me," he said. "I don't like the heat."

"You're in the wrong place then," Tree said.

Trinchera looked at him sharply. "What's that supposed to mean?"

"Just that if you want to avoid the heat, you're in the wrong place," Tree said.

"Right, okay. I got that."

"Are you all alone here?" Tree asked.

"Why would you ask that?"

"Hey, take it easy, will you? I just asked you a question."

"But why would you ask me *that* question? Why would you ask me *that* particular question?"

"Okay, listen to me, Mr. Trinchera, I'm going to ask you another question. I don't want you to get mad. I just want a simple answer."

"I don't know why you're asking me these questions." Trinchera was sitting up straight now, his body tense. "You come in here, you start asking questions. Edith never said you would be asking so many questions."

"What did Edith say?"

"She said you were a private dick. You would be able to help me out."

"That's what I'm trying to do, but I don't know anything about you, Mr. Trinchera."

"I'm a Montreal businessman. That's what I am. My brother and me, we own some funeral homes in Montreal. Who says different?"

"Nobody, as far as I know."

"Okay, then. As long as that's understood."

"Is there any reason why three men, maybe sent by a guy name Johnny, would be coming for you?"

The suspicion was back in Trinchera's eyes. "What's that? What are you talking about?"

"Tell me."

"You say three guys? Coming here?"

"They could be, yes. They were at the Biltmore Hotel a few minutes ago. One of them was reassuring Johnny on the phone that they were coming here for you, and that everything was going to be taken care of. He said he was in the business of breaking eggs."

Beneath the peak of the Greek fisherman's cap, Vic Trinchera's hollowed-out eyes filled with worry. "You sure that's what he said?"

"Whoever was on the other end of the phone apparently wanted an egg broken. This guy said he knew how to break an egg. That's what he said."

"You didn't bring those rats here, did you?"

"No, of course not," Tree said.

"You working for Johnny Bravo, is that it?"

"Johnny Bravo? Who's Johnny Bravo? I'm not working for anyone. What's going on here? Are you in trouble?"

"No," Trinchera said, his voice rising. "Why would I be in trouble? I'm a Montreal businessman, I tell you. That's all there is to it."

Trinchera pulled himself out of the recliner and rose unsteadily to his feet. He looked as though a strong breeze would blow him away.

"A businessman, trying to enjoy his time in Florida, that's all there is to it. It's this heat. I can't stand this heat."

He fumbled in his pocket, finally extracting a cellphone. "These damned things," he said angrily.

"What are you doing?" Tree demanded.

"Shut up," Vic Trinchera said.

He poked out a number and then spoke into the phone "Yeah, it's me," he said. "I need you to bring a car around. Right now."

He put the cellphone away and inspected Tree. Having made the phone call, he appeared less agitated. His voice when he spoke was calmer. "You sure Johnny didn't send you?"

"I told you, I don't even know who Johnny Bravo is."

"A ruthless son of a bitch is who he is," Trinchera said. The agitation was back.

"I don't even know who you are."

"How many times do I have to tell you? A respectable Montreal businessman. They gave me some sort of award a couple of years ago. They don't give you no award if you're not respectable."

"That's good. If you're respectable you don't have to worry. You don't need me."

"I need a detective."

"Retired," Tree said. "I'm retired from that business. Edith should have told you."

"Every creep in this state is retired. I don't need retired. I need a detective."

"For what?"

Trinchera bobbed his head up and down. "Okay, I don't have a lot of choice here. I can't trust anyone I know. Anyone I know would as soon cut my throat as look at me. Even that broad. Can't trust her, either."

"Broad?" Tree said the word as though it came from some all-but-lost ancient language. "What broad? What are you talking about?"

The old man ignored him. "Edith sent you. I guess you're okay. I don't know, anymore. I don't know about anything. I used to be able to trust certain people. But that's all gone now. So I need you to take the dog."

"Dog?" Tree said. "What dog?"

"The dog." Trinchera's irritation had turned into anger. "The dog you're supposed to take care of."

"Edith didn't say anything about a dog," Tree said.

"I'm trusting you. I don't have any choice. I gotta get out of here. You're taking the dog."

Tree was on his feet. "I came down here to talk, that's all. Nothing was said about any dog."

"What kind of punk are you?" Trinchera's long, gray face was darkening. "You're retired. You don't take dogs. You don't do this. You don't do that. Don't give me this crap, understand? I don't have time for it."

He lurched away, and as he did, his cellphone began to ring. "Are you there yet?" he snarled into the phone. "Hold on, I'll be right out."

He disappeared down a corridor. Tree thought now was a good time to get out. This old guy was obviously deranged. Whatever possessed Edith to send him on this wild goose chase?

Before Tree could do anything, Trinchera reappeared pulling a leash attached to a floppy-eared hound. Brown patches intersected white fur on a slim, arched body held by spindly legs attached to the world's biggest paws. A brown and white kitty plush toy was lodged between the dog's jaws.

"This is Clinton," Trinchera announced.

Clinton looked up at Tree with big hound dog eyes before giving the plush toy in his mouth a good shake.

"He's a hound," Tree said.

"A *French* hound," Trinchera corrected.

"I didn't know there was such a thing," Tree said. "Why would you call a French hound Clinton?"

"I like Bill Clinton, what can I tell you? Here, give me that." Trinchera reached down and before the dog could stop him, he swiped the kitten plush toy away. Clinton yelped and jumped up, tail wagging furiously, anxious to get his toy back. Vic held the toy above his head and at the same time handed Tree the leash.

"Hang onto him for a minute. I gotta get rid of this."

Trinchera, holding the plush toy, darted out of sight. Clinton strained at his leash, desperate to follow, making whimpering sounds. "It's all right, boy," Tree said. "Just stay where you are."

He patted the dog's head and Clinton dropped to his haunches, panting excitedly, closely watching the door through which Trinchera had exited.

A moment later, the old man was back saying, "Okay, so you got the dog, and you know his name. He eats two meals a day. Just feed him dry kibble. He likes that. Anything else you need?"

"What are you talking about?" Tree said in alarm. "I can't take this dog."

"What? You don't like Bill Clinton? You've got something against French hounds?"

Trinchera turned to a side table next to the couch. Clinton wagged his tail, and regarded Tree with his sad eyes. Trinchera opened a drawer and withdrew a gun.

"What's that?" Tree demanded.

"What's it look like?" Vic Trinchera said.

He pointed the gun at the dog.

"Here's the thing," Trinchera said. "You either take this dog off my hands in the next two minutes, or I'm gonna shoot him."

Clinton's head turned at an angle, those big eyes fixed on Tree.

"Come on," Tree said. "You're not going to shoot a dog right here in your living room."

"If that's what you think, you don't know me," Trinchera said.

"This is crazy," Tree said.

Outside, Tree heard the sound of a car. "No time left," Vic Trinchera announced. "I gotta go." He glared at Tree as if Tree were responsible for all this. "Take him. He'll lead you to places you never imagined. What's it going to be, Mr. Private Detective?"

Tree looked at the dog. He looked at the gun. He took note of the grim set of Vic Trinchera's face, and understood in a flash that the old man was just crazy enough, desperate enough—whatever—to pull the trigger.

"Did you say you feed him kibble?" Tree said.

"A bowl, twice a day. Make sure he gets plenty of exercise."

Trinchera shoved his gun into the belt of his pants and then started toward the door.

"Hey, wait a minute," Tree called after him. "Where do you think you're going?"

But Vic was already out the door, slamming it behind him. A moment later, he heard the sound of a car heading away from the house.

Tree, holding the leash, turned and looked at the dog. Clinton's jaws dropped open, his tongue flopped into view; an irresistible hound dog smile.

4

Tree got lost trying to get onto the Palmetto Expressway. He hated himself when he did this, hated the lousy sense of direction everyone accused him of having, when in fact he always knew where he was going.

Except today.

Today, making his way out of Miami, he was—well, he was having some difficulty.

In the back seat, Clinton moved around restlessly. He seemed nervous at being in this unfamiliar vehicle with a stranger behind the wheel. Occasionally, he made whimpering sounds. Tree tried to reassure him. "Listen," he called back, shooting a glance at the rear-view mirror. "If it weren't for me, who knows what would have happened to you."

The dog settled on his haunches for a time, then rose up, gave himself a good shake and then twisted back and forth in the cramped back seat. Tree tried comforting him again.

Clinton did not seem reassured.

The traffic at this time of day was stop-and-go. It took Tree forever to ease back onto the expressway. That's when everything came to a dead stop. Miami traffic was bad, but usually it wasn't this bad. Tree gritted his teeth. Welcome to driving anywhere in the twenty-first century. Ahead, he could see motorists, their cars stopped, get out and lean over the barrier at the edge of the highway, peering down onto Coral Way.

Curious about what was happening, Tree got out of the Beetle and walked to join a knot of motorists focused on the highway below. Coral Way had been blocked off, and there were a dozen blue and white City of Miami police cars and emergency vehicles parked helter-skelter around a black Cadillac Escalade that had come to rest beside one of the overpass restraining walls. He could make out what looked like three holes in the passenger side window.

"Any idea what happened?" he said to a short, pudgy man wearing a Florida Marlins baseball cap.

"Shooting of some sort, apparently," the man in the baseball cap said. "Hey, it's Miami, right?"

Below, a police officer approached the Cadillac and gingerly opened the door. As soon as he did, something fell out onto the pavement. The officer quickly stooped to pick it up. But before he did, Tree got a look at it.

A Greek fisherman's cap.

As he struggled out of Miami rush-hour traffic, local radio reported that there had been a shooting on Coral Way. Police were saying little except that one man was pronounced dead at the scene.

One man wearing a Greek fisherman's cap?

Tree tried to assure himself that there were lots of men in Miami wearing Greek fisherman's caps, and that the odds of one of those men being Vic Trinchera were not great.

Or were they?

After all, how many other men in Greek fisherman's caps had gone running out the door to avoid three dangerous-looking characters coming to do exactly what had been done to the guy on Coral Way?

Just before he turned onto Alligator Alley, Tree called Edith Goldman. He got her voice mail. "I'm not sure what's going on, Edith," Tree said. "Call me as soon as you get this. We need to talk."

As he started to punch out Freddie's number, Clinton in the back, considerably settled since they left Miami, squeezed his head between the seats and nuzzled Tree's hand. "I'm not going to pet you," Tree said to the dog. "If I start to pet you, I'm going to get attached to you, and that's a mistake."

Clinton responded by pushing at his hand. "I can't have a dog in my life," Tree went on. "I'm supposed to be simplifying things, not making them more complicated."

Tree put the phone down and reached back to stroke the dog's snout while he drove. "Don't get the idea I'm a pushover for you or anything like that," Tree admonished. "Your real problem, as you will soon discover, is my wife, Freddie. How she's going to react to your arrival is anyone's guess."

"At least I can hear you," Freddie said when she came on the line. "Where are you?"

"I've got a dog," Tree said.

"Where's I've-got-a-dog?" Freddie asked.

"It's not a place," Tree said. "It's a dog."

"I'm having trouble with this line again. I could have sworn you said something about a dog."

"I've got one—we've got one. A dog, I mean."

"Tree, we can't have a dog."

"The guy was going to shoot him."

"What?

"Vic Trinchera. The guy. He pulled out a gun and put it to Clinton's head. He would have pulled the trigger if I hadn't agreed to take him."

"Who is Clinton?" Freddie sounded exasperated.

"Clinton is the name of the dog. He's a French hound."

"A French hound named Clinton?"

"After President Clinton."

"Don't come home with a dog," Freddie said.

Then she hung up.

"You see the kind of trouble you've got me in," Tree said to the dog. "Now what am I going to do with you?"

He felt Clinton's damp nose nuzzle against the back of his arm. "Don't think that's going to do you any good," Tree said.

Clinton nuzzled again, and, of course, that was all it took for Tree not to think twice about driving to the first Pet Valu he spotted off the highway. He bought a bag of Iams kibble, two large aluminum bowls, dog bone treats, a dog bed, extra-large, as well as a yellow ball. Clinton accompanied Tree along the aisles, wagging his tail in encouragement.

When they finally reached Andy Rosse Lane, Tree led Clinton inside the house and unsnapped his leash. The dog spent the next few minutes sniffing around the kitchen and living room, acclimatizing himself to his new space. Meanwhile, Tree poured kibble into one bowl and filled the other with water. He placed the bowls on the floor. Clinton sauntered over, sniffed at the kibble and then continued on with his inspection tour.

Freddie arrived home an hour or so later. As soon as she walked in the door, Clinton's head shot up, his ears arched, and he uttered a loud, decisive howl.

"What big ears he has," Freddie said.

"At least you didn't say 'get rid of that dog,'" Tree said.

"I'm barely in the door. Give me a moment."

Clinton lowered his head and then came over to Freddie, the nails of his paws clicking against the kitchen tile, his tail wagging furiously. "I'm not going to pet him," Freddie said.

"That's what I said," Tree said.

"If I pet him, that's it. I'm lost."

"Join the club," Tree said.

Freddie reached out a tentative hand. Clinton lifted his head to meet her hand. "He has such soft fur," Freddie said. Her hand slid back and forth along his forehead and then moved down to scratch his ears. Clinton turned his head and closed his eyes. "He likes that," Freddie said. She looked at Tree. "What are we going to do with him?"

"I've got to get hold of Edith and find out what's going on," Tree said. "She never said anything about babysitting a dog. She also didn't say anything about three toughs who might be looking for a guy who is supposed to be a law-abiding Montreal businessman."

"Tree, you are retired. Remember?"

"I am retired," Tree said, as much to convince himself as Freddie.

Clinton had returned to his kibble for another sniff while Freddie retreated to the refrigerator and a bottle of chardonnay. Tree told her about stopping at the Biltmore Hotel and his encounter with three men who appeared to be planning something for Trinchera. "As soon as I told Vic about these guys, he left the house in a car, leaving me with the dog."

"Did these characters show up?"

"Not before I got out of there," Tree said.

"So it could be nothing," Freddie said. "It could be that these men were business associates or something."

"If they were, why didn't Vic stick around? The old guy got out of there pretty fast, let me tell you."

Freddie poured white wine into a long-stemmed glass. "I can't believe Edith got you involved in this."

"Whatever 'this' is."

"It involves thugs and a disappearing old guy—not good."

"And a dog."

"Yes, a dog." Freddie sipped her wine. "The hound of the Sanibel Sunset detective."

"Only temporarily." Tree looked at Clinton, engrossed in gulping down his kibble. "I'll get hold of Edith and then get the dog back to his owner. No problem."

Freddie stopped sipping her wine. "I hate it when you say that."

"Say what?"

"When you say 'no problem.'"

"Why do you hate it?"

"Because," Freddie said, "whenever you say there is 'no problem,' there is inevitably a problem."

As Tree and Freddie undressed for bed later that night, Clinton poked his head through the door, inquisitively inspecting his new hosts. Tree sighed and went into the kitchen and retrieved Clinton's bed and brought it into the bedroom. Freddie was already in bed, her back to him, announcing, "I'm dead."

"I know you are," he said.

He placed the dog bed on the floor. Clinton raised a paw and poked at it a couple of times before springing onto Tree and Freddie's bed with unexpected agility. He sat back on his haunches, lowered his head so that his ears fell forward. Then he began to bite at them.

"What's he doing?" Freddie murmured, her eyes closed.

"He's playing with his ears," Tree said.

That brought Freddie up on her elbow, watching Clinton gnaw at his ears.

"I don't believe it," she said. "The dog is playing with his ears."

"It's too bad they cancelled the *Ed Sullivan Show*," Tree said.

"Tree, he shouldn't be on the bed," Freddie said.

Clinton tired of playing with his ears, lowered himself onto the mattress, dropping his head between his paws, those big, doleful eyes on Tree.

"It's his first night here," Tree said. "He's probably feeling stressed, a new environment and everything. We should do all we can to put him at ease."

"You're too much of a softy." Freddie had lain down again. She already sounded as though she was drifting off.

"Not me," Tree said. "I'm hard as nails."

He turned off the light and then crawled into bed. Clinton snuggled against him. Tree reached out and put his arm around Freddie. "I love you."

"I love you, too, my darling," Freddie confirmed. A moment later she was sound asleep.

Tree lay in the darkness, his arm still around his wife, feeling the weight of Clinton against him, thinking about the day's events, worrying he had not heard from Edith. Maybe he was imagining things, as Freddie suggested. Maybe the three men at the hotel were not after Vic Trinchera. But then why would Vic threaten to shoot his own dog, then disappear, and what— get himself killed on the side of a Miami highway?

The television news hadn't been much help. Late that night, according to the reporter covering the story, Miami Police still had not identified the man who had been shot in the Cadillac Escalade on Coral Way. As Tree turned on his side, he clung to the hope that the dead man wasn't Vic Trinchera. Clinton shifted so that he nestled into the crook of his new pal's legs. What were they going to do about a dog? Tree thought. Not to worry. He would get in touch with Edith, and she would find out what had happened to Vic Trinchera. Except even if Vic were alive, he appeared capable of shooting Clinton, and Tree could not imagine that. No one was going to shoot this dog if he had anything to do with it.

As he drifted off, Tree was filled with a sensation he had not experienced in a long time, an intense feeling of well-being. He could hardly believe it. It must be something else. It could not be the dog.

Except it was.

So Charles Schulz was right.

Happiness is a warm puppy.

5

When the alarm went off at its usual six o'clock time the next morning, Tree came slowly awake to discover Freddie already sitting up—staring down at Clinton stretched out against Tree, dead to the world.

"You've got to be kidding," Freddie said.

"What?" Tree struggled up, trying not to disturb the sleeping Clinton.

"The dog slept with us last night."

"You knew that."

"I thought I was dreaming."

Clinton stirred, lifted his head, and then squirmed around until he was lying on his back between the two of them, his legs in the air.

"He wants you to stroke his stomach," Tree said.

"I am not stroking this dog's stomach," Freddie said.

Clinton squirmed some more. Freddie sighed before reaching out a tentative hand and rubbing it along his belly. Clinton moved his head back so that his throat was exposed. He looked ecstatic.

"We can't do this," Freddie said, continuing to pet him.

"We can't do what?"

"We can't allow ourselves to become attached to this dog."

"We're not attached."

"Yes, we are, Tree, and he's not our dog. You're going to have to give him back."

"I know that," Tree said.

"I don't think you do," Freddie said.

She stopped petting Clinton, and he rolled onto his side. She took another look at him, shook her head, and then got out of bed. "I'm going to take a shower," she said.

Tree got up and stretched. His sciatic nerve was throbbing, and he had trouble walking on his left foot thanks to what he had learned was plantar fasciitis caused by the wear and tear of morning beach runs on the ligament connecting the heel bone to his toes. He hobbled into the kitchen, Clinton following eagerly.

Tree finished making the coffee as Freddie, right on cue, entered wearing a pale linen pantsuit. As he did each morning, Tree marveled at her exquisitely cut blond hair, the dazzling green of those eyes, the subtle, sensual elegance of a beauty age had failed so miserably to defeat. He wondered, as he wondered at some point every day, how he had ever been lucky enough to marry her—how she had been crazy enough to marry him.

He handed her a coffee cup, accompanied by a kiss on the mouth. Clinton sniffed around the kitchen, reconfirming his new surroundings. Freddie watched him as she sipped her coffee. Tree noticed she could not help smiling.

"See?" he said. "You like him. You can't help but like him."

"Of course I like him," Freddie said putting her coffee on the counter, half finished. "He's a big, lovely, affectionate guy—somewhat like my husband. I just don't want to like him too much." She kissed Tree's mouth. "The dog, I mean. Not the husband."

"I'm glad you clarified that for me," Tree said.

"I've got to get going. What are you up to today?"

"I'm retired, remember? Maybe I'll wander around and see if I can find a shuffleboard game somewhere."

Freddie rolled her eyes and gave him another kiss. "You are going to do something about the dog, aren't you?"

"I'll get in touch with Edith and see if I can get to the bottom of what's going on."

"Please don't get yourself mixed up in anything you shouldn't be mixed up in," Freddie said.

"I never do."

"Liar." At least she said it affectionately, Tree thought. Didn't she?

———————

Tree poured more kibble into a bowl and set it on the floor. This time Clinton didn't bother with food inspection but dug right into it while Tree went into the bedroom and changed into a T-shirt and shorts. He waited until Clinton finished off the bowl and then put him on his leash and the two of them proceeded out onto Andy Rosse Lane and down to the beach at the end of the street.

Tree thought about it, and then unhooked Clinton's leash from the bright yellow collar he wore around his neck. "Okay, now I trust you not to run away," he said to the dog. Clinton, busily sniffing the sand, did not appear to be listening.

Tree broke into a run. Clinton, ears flapping, bounded along beside him.

It was another one of those perfect sun-drenched mornings Tree had begun to take for granted, except today was even better, out here on the beach, his sciatic nerve calm, the pain momentarily gone from his foot tendons, splashing in the surf, with one's beloved canine companion.

Except Clinton wasn't exactly his, as Freddie was quick to remind him. That caused Tree to slow his pace while Clinton raced on, those giant paws kicking up tufts of sand. Clinton was just a dog, after all. Tree would care for him as long as necessary and then give him up and that would be that.

How could it be anything else? The last thing he and Freddie wanted in their lives right now was a dog—even if they could have Clinton.

Which they couldn't.

His cellphone rumbled and vibrated in his pocket. He pulled the phone out. It was Edith. At once he was relieved and crushed. For a crazy moment, he debated whether to take the call. Then he swiped the phone open.

"Edith," he said. "I've been trying to get hold of you."

"Haven't you heard?" Edith's voice sounded tense.

"Heard what?"

"They found Vic's body yesterday."

Tree felt his stomach sinking. "Where did they find him?"

"They found him in his car on the side of the highway in Miami."

He decided to play dumb. "What was it? A heart attack?"

"It was his heart all right. Someone put a bullet in it."

"You're kidding."

"I am," Edith said. "They actually put three bullets in it."

Tree had a flash of the Cadillac Escalade on the side of Coral Way. The police officer picking up the Greek fisherman's cap.

"Tree?" Edith's insistent voice. "Are you still there?"

"Yes, I'm still here, Edith."

"The dog," she said.

"The dog?"

"What did you do with Vic's dog?"

Clinton, noticing Tree was no longer following, had paced back. He stopped a few feet in front of Tree, tail twitching. He cocked his head as though to inquire why Tree wasn't running.

Before he could even think about lying, he lied: "What dog?"

"What do you mean 'what dog?'" Edith sounded even more exasperated. "Didn't Vic give you his dog to look after?"

"That's why you sent me down there? So I could babysit a dog?"

"Tree, did he give you the dog or not?"

"No," Tree said.

"I'm going to have to call you back," Edith said.

"Edith, don't hang up. Tell me what's going on."

Edith hung up.

Tree put his phone away and looked at Clinton. "What have I just done?" he said to the dog. "I just lied through my teeth about you, and I'm not sure why I did it."

Clinton responded with a bark, and then gave Tree another inquiring look, as if curious as to what his pal thought of his bark. Then he turned and resumed his inspection along the beach.

"What's even worse," Tree said, calling after him, "I'm talking to a dog."

Clinton put his head down and began sniffing at the surf.

"Did you hear me?" Tree yelled. "I'm talking to a dog!"

6

By the time Tree arrived back at the house with Clinton, he was beginning to have serious second thoughts about what he had told Edith. Vic Trinchera was dead, shot to death shortly after he drove away from Tree. Not only was he in possession of the dead man's dog, he also had important information pertaining to the crime—namely, the three characters he had overheard at the hotel discussing what now appeared to be Vic's impending demise.

He should phone Edith back. He should talk to the police.

But he did neither of those things.

And he still wasn't quite certain why—until he looked at Clinton and Clinton looked back at him with those big sad eyes as if to say, "You're it, pal. You're all I've got. So you have to protect me."

Tree shook himself back to reality. Stop this, he thought to himself. Clinton was a *dog*. He wasn't really saying anything.

Really.

But then again, he was. In his own way.

Tree turned on the television and gritted his teeth through the inane puffery of the *Today* show, waiting for the local news on the half hour. Vic Trinchera's death led off the newscast.

The youthful news anchor said, "Canada's Mafia wars apparently have spilled over into South Florida with the murder yesterday of wealthy Montreal mortician Victor Trinchera. Police say that Trinchera for many years was the powerful, ruthless head of a Montreal crime family."

Video footage showed the Cadillac with a figure slumped in the front seat. Three bullet holes in the passenger side window were clearly visible.

"Trinchera's body was found yesterday afternoon on Coral Way not far from his home in Coral Gables. He had been shot three times. Police don't have any suspects. We reached Canadian crime specialist and author James Devereaux in Montreal."

A blond-haired professorial-looking man appeared on the screen. The news anchor said, "Thanks for speaking to us this morning. We appreciate it. Tell us about this Vic Trinchera."

Devereaux arranged an expression on his face that one adopts for television—an expression that says you know what you are talking about. "Trinchera had recently been involved in a feud with his rival, Johnny Rizzo, known as Johnny Bravo," Devereaux said. "You have to believe this hit is related to their feud. If that's the case, you may not have seen the last of Canadian gangster violence in Miami."

"Jim, we don't usually think of gangsters when we think of Canada. What gives, anyway?"

"We've got bad guys here, just like you," Devereaux said. "Montreal has a particularly rich history of organized crime, not just the Mafia but biker gangs, too."

"Now they're coming down here?"

"Gangsters are like most Canadians, they like the Florida weather in winter. What's a bit surprising is that they've started to kill each other down there."

The anchor turned to his female co-anchor, a woman with shimmering blond hair. The anchor said, "Isn't that great, Merilee? As if we didn't have enough trouble with our own gangsters right here in Miami, now we've got the Canadians shooting one another."

"I thought Canadians were polite, ate peameal bacon, and watched hockey," Merilee said. Then she announced to the camera: "Canadian bad guys stay home." She smiled, displaying the world's whitest teeth. "Only kidding. We love Canadians, of course!"

"Except the ones with guns," the young anchor said. "And what's peameal bacon?"

"I'm not sure, but Canadians eat it," said Merilee.

Terrific, Tree thought. He had gotten himself mixed up with a Canadian gangster—a dead Canadian gangster. What was Edith thinking?

The anchors did not linger on peameal bacon or bad news. The weather was a more reliable topic on local newscasts. A hot, sunny weekend was in the offing. Whatever bad things happened, they would happen in the sunshine.

Clinton bounced up onto the sofa and eased himself down beside Tree, laying his head on Tree's lap. "Are you a Mafia dog, Clinton?" Tree asked. "Is that what you are? What kind of trouble have you landed me in?"

If Clinton could answer, Tree reasoned, the dog might point out that he hadn't landed Tree in trouble. Tree had done that all by himself.

As usual.

"Can you even say Mafia anymore?" he said to Clinton. "Is that politically correct? Maybe I should not use the word Mafia. Maybe you are an organized-crime dog."

Clinton regarded him with baleful eyes—the long-suffering organized-crime dog in need of affection. Tree gave him a pat. Clinton once again began playfully biting at the ends of his ears.

He thought about phoning Edith back, and then decided against it. As much as he wanted to ask her what she was doing mixed up with a Canadian gangster, he didn't want to tell her any more lies than he already had. He was supposed to be out of the business of lying. He hadn't lasted a day before he was right back at it.

His phone sounded. Fearing it was Edith, he pulled the phone from his pocket and checked the readout. It wasn't Edith, but he didn't recognize the number.

"Is this Walter Tremain Callister?" An official-sounding female voice.

"Who is this?"

"Yes, well, is this Walter Tremain Callister?" The female voice sounded less certain of itself.

"Yes," Tree said. "Who's calling?"

"Good, so you are Mr. Callister." A pause. "Mr. Callister, I'm Sergeant Melora Spark . . ."

"Sergeant? Sergeant of what?"

"Of the Royal Canadian Mounted Police."

"The what?" Tree said.

"The RCMP," Melora Spark said. "That is the acronym for the Royal Canadian Mounted Police. I am a member of Canada's national police force."

"Sergeant Spark, is it?"

"That's correct, Mr. Callister." The voice in identifying itself had regained some authority.

Tree said, "It's not every day I get a call from a Canadian police officer. What can I do for you?"

"Do for me? Okay, what I would like, I would like to have a word with you if I might."

"What about?"

Sergeant Spark said, "What about? Yes, well, I would prefer not to talk about this on the phone. Do you mind—would it be possible to come to your house so we could talk there?"

He looked at Clinton contentedly attacking his ears. The last thing he wanted right now was a lot of fumbling around trying to explain the dog. "First of all, I'd like to know what this is about," Tree said.

"What it's about? Okay, it's in connection with a case I'm working on. As I told you, I would prefer not to discuss it on the phone."

"Tell you what," Tree said. "Why don't we meet at the Bubble Room? That's just around the corner from where I am, and right now a little more convenient. Do you know where it is on Captiva?"

"The Bubble Room. That's fine. I can find it, Mr. Callister. Shall we say in one hour?"

"An hour? You must be in a hurry."

"Hurry? Yes. I have a limited amount of time here. Can we meet in an hour?"

"I'll meet you at the main entrance," Tree said.

"That's fine," Melora Spark said, and hung up.

Tree looked down at Clinton. "Now what? In addition to being a French hound and an organized-crime dog, you are also a Canadian. So what is it, Clinton? Are the Canadians after you as well?"

Clinton continued to nip at his ears, apparently having the time of his life.

Tree was still holding the phone when it vibrated in his hand. Clinton stopped biting his ears His head jerked up. Tree grinned. "Sorry about this, Clinton. The phone didn't ring nearly so much before I retired."

"How's retirement?" Rex Baxter said. "Are you bored out of your mind yet?"

"What? You can't live without me?"

"Are you kidding? You've been gone less than forty-eight hours and already tourism is up."

"I think you miss me."

"Not me. Are you coming to Fun Friday tonight?"

"Right, it is Friday, isn't it?"

"See? Already you're losing track of time. That's not a good sign, Tree. Are you coming or not?"

Tree looked at Clinton. "I don't know. I hadn't thought much about it."

"Do me a favor and be there, okay?"

"Any particular reason?"

"There's someone I want you and Freddie to meet."

7

The Bubble Room was an island landmark. A maze of small rooms strung with Christmas tree lights, crammed with framed reminders of a pop culture era when Roy Rogers and Buster Crabbe and Gordon Scott (Tarzan of the movies when Tree was a kid) ruled, crowded with customers who could still recognize a languid Kim Novak or an intense Fred MacMurray, a somber Claudette Colbert (hand held against her heart) or recall when Dean Martin and Jerry Lewis co-starred in *Sailor Beware* and weren't surprised to see William Holden in a forgotten piece of nonsense called *Boots Malone*.

Tree studied the photographs in the Bubble Room's foyer. None of the staff knew who any of these people were, of course. Everyone was too young. They barely recognized the youthful John Travolta in *Saturday Night Fever*.

The front door opened and in came a slim, frazzled-looking woman, blond hair pulled back into a pony tail, the austere air of the spinsterish grade ten teacher who gave you detentions because you didn't have your English grammar homework done. Her mouth grimaced anxiously as she looked around. When she spotted Tree, she said, "There you are. Mr. Callister."

"Melora Spark?"

A quick, nervous smile. "Sergeant Melora Spark."

A frilly white blouse and unfashionable powder blue slacks did nothing to take away from the uneasy sense Tree experienced in high school when he hadn't done his homework. Only the open-toed sandals displaying small, beautifully pedicured feet provided any fashion sense.

Tree shook the pale hand she offered and said, "Sergeant Spark."

Sergeant Spark's eyes—the same color as her slacks, Tree noticed—darted around the foyer, taking in the Christmas tree lights, the walls of photos. "My goodness, this is quite a place, isn't it?" she said.

"There's nothing quite like it," Tree said.

"No, I suppose not."

A hostess led them to a corner table in one of the back rooms and presented them with menus the size of the tablets in Cecil B. DeMille's *The Ten Commandments*, a movie Tree had yet to find represented on the walls of the Bubble Room.

Melora Spark glanced perfunctorily at the menu and then put it to one side. She cleared her throat and said, "Thank you for agreeing to meet me, Mr. Callister."

"I don't want to start this off on the wrong foot or anything," Tree said.

Sergeant Spark's mouth produced more grimaces, and those blue eyes looked abruptly worried. "Wrong foot? What wrong foot?"

"Do you mind if I see some identification?" Tree said.

A waitress in a khaki Boy Scout uniform arrived, all smiles and brisk energy. "Hi, there folks. I'm Kim, and I'm your server today. Have you been to the Bubble Room before?"

Tree admitted that he had, while Melora Spark looked pained as she fumbled in her shoulder bag.

"What can I get you folks to drink?" Kim asked.

Melora blinked a couple of times and asked for a glass of water. Tree ordered a Diet Coke. "Okay, folks. Let me give you a couple of minutes with the menu, and I'll be back with your drinks."

Kim departed and Sergeant Spark slid a silver badge across the table in Tree's direction. The badge was emblazoned with a crest. Above the crest was the word POLICE. Beneath the crest: RCMP and GRC.

What's GRC stand for?" Tree wanted to know.

"Gendarmerie Royale du Canada," she promptly replied. "That's French."

"I see," Tree said.

"Canada being a bilingual country."

"Yes, of course."

She cleared her throat again and said, "Maintiens le droit. That's French, too. Defending the law. Our motto, you see."

"Is that what brings you to Florida? You're here defending the law?"

She flashed a quick, nervous smile. "That's a joke, right? I understand that. I'm trying to loosen up about these things. You know, 'get the joke,' as they say."

"I'm just so funny," Tree said, deadpan. "The point being, Sergeant Spark, I'm not sure how I can help you."

"That's the thing, you see, you can help me. That's why I asked to meet you."

Kim the server arrived with their drinks. "Have you folks had a chance to look at the menu yet?"

"Give us a few more minutes, will you, Kim?"

"Let me know when you're ready to order."

Tree addressed Melora. "Are you hungry?"

"No. My stomach's all funny. I didn't know we would be eating. I don't usually eat lunch." Her hands fluttered over the menu as if trying to levitate it.

"Okay, how am I supposed to help the Mounties," Tree said.

"It's the dog."

Tree looked at her. "The dog?"

Kim returned, her youthful face lighting with hope. "You folks ready yet?"

Tree sighed and looked at the menu. "What about you? Sure you don't want something?"

"I'm fine, thanks."

The menu contained luncheon dishes such as Gone Fishin' and Hook, Line and Sinker, and Anything Grows. Tree chose the Errol Fin.

"That's the grouper filet," Kim said, nodding approvingly and then went off.

Tree said, "You said something about dogs."

Melora made a face. "I don't like dogs. I have real issues with dogs."

"I'm sorry to hear that," Tree said.

She leaned forward speaking in a low voice so that the nearby diners couldn't overhear. "Mr. Callister, the Force is aware that you met with Victor Trinchera shortly before his death."

"What force?" Tree said.

"That's what the Mounted Police call themselves. The Force."

"Okay. How do you know I met with anyone?"

"We have information to that effect," she said in her police-officer-giving-testimony voice. "So what about it, Mr. Callister? What were you doing with Vic Trinchera the morning he died?"

Tree said, "My lawyer sent me to see him."

"Why would your lawyer do that?"

"She said he needed to talk to a private detective."

"Are you a private detective?"

"No, I'm not."

She looked flustered again, and spent more time clearing her throat. "Then I don't understand. Why would your lawyer send you to him?"

"She thought I was a private detective."

"But you are not."

"I'm retired."

Sergeant Spark paused before she said, "I see. But you went down there, anyway."

"That's right."

"Did you know who Mr. Trinchera was?"

"You mean did I know he was a gangster? I had no idea."

"He didn't tell you when you got to his house?"

"He didn't tell me anything. He left shortly after I arrived."

"Yes. Okay. And what did you do?"

"There was nothing else to do. I left."

"What about the dog?"

"I thought you didn't like dogs."

"I don't like them, but Vic did."

"There was no dog."

"You should know, Mr. Callister, you should know that Victor Trinchera was one of the top Mafioso in Montreal. He ran the town while his boss, Johnny Bravo, was in prison. However, when Mr. Bravo was released last year, he naturally wished to resume his position as head of the family. Vic Trinchera appeared to go along with this, but in fact was working against Mr. Bravo behind the scenes, trying to bring him down."

"So then what was Vic doing in the Miami area?" Tree asked.

"Supposedly, he was here to have open-heart surgery, but in fact it was something else entirely."

"Which was?"

"In order to avoid going to jail for an art theft he committed as a young man, Vic Trinchera agreed to work with us as an informant. He came to Miami to make peace with Johnny Bravo and hopefully get himself reinstated in the family. That way he would be more valuable to us."

"That didn't work out so well," Tree said.

"It is a big disappointment to me, and to the Force," Melora said.

"Well, I'm afraid there isn't much I can do to help you," Tree said. "I obviously wasn't aware of any of this."

"And you have no idea why Mr. Trinchera would have need of a private detective—even a retired private detective?"

"Not a clue," Tree said.

"What about your lawyer. What's her name?"

"Edith Goldman," Tree said. Finally, a question he could answer truthfully.

"Edith Goldman," Melora repeated, as if to make a mental note of it. "And Ms. Goldman does not know why Mr. Trinchera wanted to see you?"

"If she does, she didn't tell me, and since the murder of Mr. Trinchera, I've only spoken briefly to her."

"She didn't happen to say anything about a dog, did she?"

"I can only repeat what I've already told you. I don't know anything about a dog."

"You're sure. This is Vic Trinchera's dog." Melora's blue eyes focused on him, unblinking.

"A dog you don't like."

"That's beside the point."

"I didn't know he was a gangster, and I didn't know he had a dog." Tree thought the words came out of his mouth smoothly enough. During his time as a private detective, he had become quite a proficient liar, a dubious accomplishment, to say the least.

"Yes, he did. Have a dog, I mean. Now the dog is missing."

"How do you know this?"

"When I went back to get the dog—I mean I hated the idea. I don't even like to touch them. Hate the sound of their barking. Anyway, when I arrived at the house, the dog wasn't there."

"He called you, didn't he?" Tree said. "I was there when he made the call. He called the police officer he was working with when he thought his life might be in danger. You picked him up."

Melora didn't say anything. But her head moved up and down ever so slightly.

"When you drove off with Trinchera, where did you take him?"

She hesitated as though deciding whether to answer him. "To a safe place," she finally answered.

"It couldn't have been very safe," Tree said.

"Unfortunately, Mr. Trinchera didn't do as he was told. He put himself needlessly in harm's way."

"That's not so good for you, then, is it Sergeant Spark?"

Her mouth renewed its twisting, as though she had tasted something she didn't like. "It is most important we find the dog, Mr. Callister. Anything you could do to help us in that regard would be most appreciated."

"What does the dog look like?"

"The animal is a French hound."

"I've never heard of a French hound."

"Apparently, these hounds are the French equivalent of the English foxhound. They use them for hunting."

"Is that so?"

"Clinton. That's the name he answers to. Clinton."

"A French dog named Clinton?"

"Named after the U.S. president, apparently."

"What's so important about this dog?"

She regarded him with narrowed eyes. "I'm afraid I can't tell you that. But there is a substantial reward if he is found."

"What kind of substantial reward?"

"I don't know," she admitted. "I will have to check with my superiors."

"So it might not be so substantial."

"As I say, I will check with my superiors."

She placed a business card on the table. It contained the logo of the RCMP. She produced a ballpoint pen and then wrote a number on the back of the card. "This is my local cell phone. If you have more information or if you find the dog, don't hesitate to call me at any time."

She handed him her card and looked at him expectantly.

Tree said, "Like I told you, I'm retired. And now my prospective client is dead. I don't think I'm going to be much help to you."

For the first time since they met, Sergeant Melora Spark actually smiled. She had a very nice smile, Tree thought. With the smile on, she did not look so rigid and authoritarian.

The smile was gone quickly as she rose to her feet. "Please call me when you find the dog," she said.

"I'm not looking for the dog," Tree reminded her.

"I will be in touch, Mr. Callister." She collected her shoulder purse and left the restaurant.

Kim the server returned with Tree's grouper. Her smile was a bright hope for the future. "Can I get you anything else?" she asked.

8

A mournful howl rose from inside the house on Andy Rosse Lane as Tree approached. Clinton, agitated, was alerting anyone looking for him as to his whereabouts.

He waited just inside the door, full-throttle tail wagging, one of Tree's sneakers clasped between his jaws—a gift for his new pal, the forgiveness for desertion. Tree took the sneaker and thanked him with a soothing hand. "However, you're supposed to be quiet so people can't find you," he admonished. "You are not supposed to be announcing your presence to the entire island."

Clinton excitedly followed him into the kitchen. The dog had not touched his water or his food since Tree left. "What? You think I'm going to abandon you, is that it? So you're saving your food, just in case. Is that what you're doing?"

Tree opened the refrigerator for a Diet Coke while Clinton went over and sniffed at his food. He then helped himself to a long drink. The tips of his ears dipped into the water bowl.

"Here's the thing, Clinton, you don't have to worry," Tree said, leaning against the counter. "No one's going to desert you."

Seemingly satisfied with this reassurance, Clinton began to wolf down his kibble. Tree watched him, shaking his head. "But what is it about you? First your owner is anxious to give you to me. Next my lawyer wants to know where you are, and now the Canadian police are after you. What kind of dog are you, anyway?"

Tree stroked Clinton's head. Clinton looked up briefly at Tree with those big baleful eyes, and then returned to his food. Tree's cellphone rang. It was Rex Baxter.

"I just wanted to make sure you're at Fun Friday," Rex said.

"I told you I was going to be there," Tree said.

"I know what you told me," Rex said, irritably. "I just want to make sure you do it, that's all."

"It's important to you, so I'll be there."

"Maybe I just miss you, and I call you because I long to hear the dulcet tones of your voice."

"That could be it all right," Tree said.

"I'll see you in a while," Rex said, hanging up.

After Clinton finished eating, Tree took him along Andy Rosse, the hound relieving himself and marking his territory at intervals. The beach was crowded this afternoon, so Tree kept the dog on his leash. Clinton turned out to be quite the celebrity, everyone coming up and admiring this unusual dog. He's a French hound, Tree explained in response to the questions, reciting what he had discovered online. They are known as Porcelaines, the French version of the English foxhound seen in those old hunting prints.

This explanation, repeated over and over, appeared to satisfy most of Clinton's admirers, particularly children. Clinton took all this attention in stride. He permitted a little girl to play with his ears, and he waited patiently while a little boy decided whether or not he had the courage to touch his nose—patience paid off. He finally worked up the nerve, and, as he petted the dog, his face glowed with pleasure.

Tree found that he was enjoying himself, strolling along the beach beneath a late afternoon sun with this four-legged creature who overnight had become a fixture in his life. A couple of days ago, he would not even have thought of a dog. Now, he had to admit to himself, he was having trouble imagining life without one.

Back at the house, Tree changed into a pair of long pants, put on a fresh shirt, made sure Clinton had water in his bowl, and collected his keys. Clinton stood glumly watching him. When Tree opened the door, the dog tried to scramble out. Tree had to grab him by the collar. "No, boy, you stay here, okay? I'm going to be only an hour or so, and then I'll be back, and we'll go for another walk."

As Tree got into his car, he could hear Clinton howl from inside. He worried all over again that if someone was looking for the dog, Clinton was doing a good job of providing his whereabouts. By the time Tree started the Beetle up, however, Clinton had gone silent. Relieved, Tree backed the car onto Andy Rosse Lane and threaded his way down Captiva, across Blind Pass onto Sanibel Island where the traffic became congested. Even taking the back way along West Gulf Drive didn't save him much time. It was nearing six o'clock by the time he got off the crowded causeway and turned onto Port Comfort Road. The Lighthouse Restaurant parking lot at this time of night was nearly full, but he finally found a spot at the end, near the marina.

The two young women behind the reception desk greeted him with smiles that gave him hope. He went into the crowded bar. He couldn't see any sign of Freddie, but Todd Jackson, elegantly turned out as always, stood at the bar beside Rex Baxter who, for the moment, had his back to Tree. When he turned, Tree could see that Rex had his arm around an attractive woman. He recognized her with a start.

Kelly Fleming.

Anyone from Chicago would have recognized her. At one time she was the Windy City's best-known newscaster.

She was also Tree Callister's second wife.

9

Kelly produced one of her glittering smiles as he approached the bar. Kelly specialized in those smiles, her stock in trade back in the day: the smile, the charm, Kelly lighting up every room she entered, her audience immediately in the palm of her hand.

As a broadcaster, you could debate her merits, but as a charmer, Kelly Fleming had no equal. That's what had brought Tree down. He stood no chance against her full court press. However, as soon as the conquest was final, Tree swearing for once to be a good husband or at least a *better* husband, the thrill of victory soon faded. Kelly grew bored and was off in search of other rooms to light up. Tree was left in darkness; single again.

She looked great in a white skirt and fuchsia-colored knit top, he thought as he embraced her. Face a little rounder, figure slightly fuller, but Kelly still; the hair, the makeup, the jewelry, the familiar scent of Guerlain—everything pretty much unchanged.

"How have you been, Tree?" Kelly said, embracing him warmly, as if he were her best friend in the world. But then everyone was Kelly's best friend in the world.

Until you weren't.

"I'm fine, Kelly. How about you?"

"Didn't you hear?"

"Hear what?"

"I've been downsized, of course," she said brightly. Personal adversity had to be promptly admitted to, accompanied by assurance that the essential Kelly was unbowed.

"They had me anchoring news at four. Ratings were great, everyone was happy—I knew I was doomed. Sure enough.

Out on the street. Age, I assume. But what can you do, Tree? It's television. It's not *if* they cancel you, it's *when* they cancel you. What about you? Rex tells me you've upset everybody on Sanibel Island with this private detective business."

"I'm retired." Tree said it like an announcement.

Kelly looked surprised. "Retired? How can you retire?"

"People keep shooting him," Rex said. Until now, he had been silent, although that was hardly an unusual state for the men in Kelly's life. When Kelly was present, she held court, all eyes focused on her.

Still, Tree thought Rex uncharacteristically tense; but then it wasn't every day you showed up with your best friend's ex-wife. Maybe that had something to do with it.

"When you were a reporter in Chicago, I marveled that more people didn't shoot you, Tree," Kelly said with a grin. "Could be your past is finally catching up to you."

"In more ways than one," Tree couldn't help but note.

Kelly arched her eyebrows, the only indication that she had caught the irony. Freddie chose that moment to make her entrance, also no shrinking violet in the perfection department, Tree mused as he went to greet her. If there was ever a day Tree wanted Freddie to look wonderful, this was it. She did not disappoint. What's more, she could easily match Kelly's smile dazzle for dazzle.

"I've heard so much about you," Kelly said when they were introduced.

"Isn't that funny?" Freddie said. "I've heard almost nothing about you, Kelly. Tree doesn't talk much about his ex-wives."

"There are so many of them, he hardly knows where to begin," Kelly said.

Tree caught Roberto the bartender's eye and ordered Freddie a glass of chardonnay. Rex was watching him as though not certain what to make of all this. What was he expecting? Tree throwing punches? Not tonight, he decided, handing Freddie her wine. "What about you, Kelly? Would you like something?"

"No, I think I'm fine, thanks, Tree," Kelly said. "I didn't get in from Chicago until late this afternoon after we sat on the runway for an hour. So I'm kind of beat." She looked at Rex. "What do you say, Rex? Are you ready to get out of here?"

"Yes," Rex said quickly. His relief was almost palpable. He wanted this encounter, but then seemingly did not want it at all.

Tree put his hand on his friend's arm and said, "How are your contacts in Miami television these days?"

Rex looked at him. "Pretty good. Why do you ask?"

"Earlier today on WBBH they interviewed a Canadian writer named James Devereaux. I'd like to get in touch with him."

"Did you try Googling him?"

"First thing I did. But there's no phone for him. I'm hoping you might know somebody at the station who can get me his number."

"Let me see what I can do," Rex said.

"I appreciate that, Rex. Thanks."

"Although I'm not sure what that has to do with you being retired."

Freddie said to Kelly, "How long are you going to be here?"

"I'm never letting her go," Rex said. He said it with more vehemence than he probably intended.

Freddie broke the ensuing awkward silence, saying, "Well, that settles that, doesn't it?"

Clinton was waiting at the door when Tree and Freddie arrived home. He presented them with one of the high-heeled shoes Freddie could no longer wear because of the arthritis in her big toe.

"Dries Van Noten," Freddie observed, carefully removing the shoe from Clinton's jaws. "You have fine taste, Clinton, I'll give you that."

They attached Clinton's leash and walked him along Andy Rosse Lane toward Captiva Drive. Friday night, the street was jammed with tourists swarming in and out of the shops, filling the restaurants. Tree told Freddie about his lunch with Melora Spark of the Mounties.

When Clinton paused to relieve himself, Freddie said, "So how are you feeling?"

"About Melora Spark?"

"About your ex-wife with your best friend."

"I don't have a problem with it," Tree said.

"Tree, come on."

"Okay, I admit, it is a little weird. Rex introduced me to Kelly—and Rex warned me not to marry her."

"Why didn't he want you to marry her?"

"He said she was wonderful, but fickle, like most television personalities, as far as he was concerned. That what she wanted today was probably not what she would want tomorrow. He said he was giving it three years."

"Was he right?"

"No, he was absolutely wrong. I only lasted two years."

"You never really told me what happened."

Clinton started up again, tugging Tree along behind him. "It was a long time ago," Tree said. "She said there wasn't another man involved. But then it turned out there was."

"How did you find that out?"

"Rex told me."

"That she was having an affair."

"I knew she'd had an affair," Tree said. "It was Rex who told me she was *still* having an affair."

"And you don't feel bitter about any of this?"

"No, I don't. Things had to unfold a certain way. I couldn't possibly have stayed married to Kelly because I had to end up married to you. That was my destiny. So you see, everything happened just as it should have. If anything, I'm grateful to Kelly and Rex, because they brought me to you."

She took his arm and hugged against him as they walked. "You are something of a charmer, aren't you Walter Tremain Callister."

"I'm only reporting the facts as I see them—and don't call me Walter."

"Are you going to say anything to Rex?"

"I'm not sure what I would say," Tree said.

"Maybe you should warn him to stay away from Kelly," Freddie said. "Maybe she'll break his heart, the way she broke yours."

"She didn't break my heart," he protested.

Freddie gave him a look.

"Rex is a big boy. He knew Kelly before I did. And besides, all this was a long time ago. Hopefully, we've all learned a few things about relationships since then."

"Kelly, too?"

"You can live in hope," Tree said.

10

Not that he thought about Kelly much anymore, but when he did, he always remembered their third date, a Saturday night party. That would be it. He had decided he was not going to see her again.

They had met at WBBM-TV following one of his appearances on Rex Baxter's afternoon movie show, the two men discussing the many virtues of Jimmy Stewart movies, Tree relating how he had interviewed Jimmy in Ann Arbor, Michigan, as a young reporter.

After the show, they were standing together in the hallway outside the studio when Kelly Fleming came along, the popular anchor of the six o'clock newscast. Rex had introduced them. A week later, she called and asked him out to dinner. That was okay. He was flattered at the attention, but they had dated twice and nothing was really clicking. He was still licking his wounds from the breakup of his first marriage and had no energy to pursue her. Besides, she worked in television, and as far as he was concerned—although he would never say anything—that worked against her. Glamorous women in television. Not for him. Not for the hard-bitten, hard-drinking, hard-living newspaperman.

At least that's what he told himself.

She had turned up at his apartment wearing a white blouse tucked into velvet jodhpurs. For some reason the jodhpurs annoyed him. Who wore jodhpurs to a party? The evening could not end fast enough.

They had walked together around the corner through a snowy Chicago night. The party was on the second floor of a Lincoln Park townhouse crowded with journalists. Somehow, they had become separated. He wasn't that interested in spending time with her, anyway. Then one of his editors wandered over, chalky face, strands of hair dripping over his forehead. "Who *is* that woman you're with?" he demanded. Someone else came along and slapped him on the shoulder and said, "Good for you. She's wonderful."

Then the crowd seemed to part and he saw her perched on a stool, surrounded by party guests, their faces shining with interest as she chatted away. Her eye caught his—a twinkle in those eyes. And something hit him. The proverbial lightning bolt. He could hardly believe it. The woman who, a few minutes before, he had wanted to get rid of, suddenly mesmerized him. How had that happened?

All these years later, replaying that long-ago party scene as Tree lay there in the first morning light, he still wondered. Was he such an egotist that the admiration of others could drive him to fall in love in a flash with someone he started the evening intending never to see again? Or was the attraction there from the beginning, and he had managed to keep the lid on it until they got to that party? Hard to say, and at this point, he told himself, it didn't matter.

But if it didn't, why did he continue to mull it over after all this time?

Beside him, Freddie breathed softly. He reached over and touched her. Clinton was stretched out between them, sound asleep. Tree eased out of bed. Clinton stirred, rolling onto his side, but continuing to sleep.

In the kitchen, Tree debated whether to make coffee, decided to wait until Freddie was awake. There was the click of paws on the hardwood floor a moment before Clinton appeared in the kitchen, tail wagging, ready for his morning walk. Tree sighed, remembering yet again—not that he needed much reminding—that when you had a dog, your life was no longer your own. Your life was your dog's life. He bent down and scratched Clinton's ears. "Well, that's not so bad, is it, baby dog? There are worse things in this world than having to take care of you."

Clinton did not seem to disagree.

Tree got into shorts and a T-shirt, slipped on a pair of sneakers and then hooked an impatient Clinton to his leash. Out they went into the cloudless morning, Tree's feeling of well-being quickly replaced by a wave of anxiety. He looked down Andy Rosse Lane, fearing he and the dog might be attacked by the Montreal Mafioso. But the street at this time of day was nearly deserted. Clinton charged toward the end of the street, seemingly not at all embarrassed to be pulling along an awkward, stumbling human.

"I don't know whether you're aware of it, but there's a dog at the end of that leash." Tree turned in the direction the voice had come from. Rex Baxter stood behind him.

"You're kidding me," Tree said.

"I would never kid you, Tree. At least not this early in the morning."

Tree pulled Clinton to a stop and waited for Rex to amble over.

"Here's where I haven't been doing my homework," Rex said. "I didn't know you had a leash, let alone a dog on the end of it."

"You're not supposed to know I've got a leash," Tree said.

"What about the dog?"

"Or a dog."

"There is simply no end to the secrets I have to keep," Rex said.

"What are you doing out here at this time of the morning, anyway?"

"I got that number you were asking about."

He reached into his pocket and passed Tree a folded slip of paper. "You can reach this Devereaux in Montreal."

"Thanks, Rex. But you could have just called me."

"I know, but it was also a good excuse to take a walk on the beach, thinking about life, trying to get things straight in my head."

"If that's the case, we might as well walk together," Tree said.

"We might at that," Rex said. He fell into step as Tree allowed Clinton to pull him forward. "What's the dog's name?"

"His name is Clinton. He's a French hound."

They came out onto the beach. A tiny band of strollers, mostly male, their faces hidden behind floppy hats and baseball caps, disturbed the egrets fluttering away in alarm. Rex eyed Clinton crossing the sand, straining at his leash.

"Clinton," Rex said. "That's a funny name for a French hound. Shouldn't his name be Pierre?"

"Maybe so. But it's Clinton."

"After the president?"

"Could be," Tree said. "But don't ask me what I'm doing with him."

"No? Why not?"

"Put it this way, the less you know about any of this, the better."

"Funny how I end up asking you the same question over and over again."

"What question is that?"

"Are you sure you know what the hell you are doing?"

"I suppose I could ask you the same question," Tree said.

"Actually, I came here to apologize to you."

"Why would you have to apologize to me?"

Clinton had paused to mark his spot at the remains of a pinkish seashell.

"I should have told you about Kelly. I shouldn't have sprung it on you like that. I don't know what I was thinking."

"Rex, it doesn't matter."

"Yeah, well, I don't know about that. I saw the look on your face when you walked into the Lighthouse last night."

"What look was that?"

"A look that said it *matters*."

"Let me ask you this, Rex. Are you happy with Kelly?"

"Never been happier," Rex said.

"Then that's all that matters."

"I loved her a long time ago, you know," Rex said, as though this was information of which Tree should have been aware.

"You told me not to marry her," Tree said.

"That's because *I* wanted her. I was jealous of you. I didn't think the two of you were right for each other."

"Well, you were right about that."

"I've thought about her a lot over the years, never really stopped thinking, if you want to know the truth. So there I was back in Chicago, and you know how they have the local Emmy Awards, and I still get invited to some of the parties. I was in the Hilton at this party and Kelly arrived. She still looked great and of course had that charm going full blast. We started talking, and then we just never stopped talking." He paused, then added, "I don't want to be alone, Tree. I'm tired of it. I'm tired of being lonely all the time."

"I know, Rex."

"So here we are."

"Walking on the beach."

"With a dog I'm not supposed to know anything about."

"He belongs to a dead gangster."

"I thought the less I know the better."

"That's true, but I have to tell someone, so I'm telling you."

"I thought you were retired."

"I am."

"Then what are you doing with a dead gangster's dog?"

"I'm not sure," Tree said. "I'm not sure how I get into the messes I get myself into—which may explain my marriage to Kelly. But as usual I'm in the mess, and now all I have to do is figure out how to get out of it."

"While you're figuring it out, I just want you to know I'm still your friend and I'm right here for you," Rex said.

"I'm glad to hear that," Tree said.

"But you should also know I plan to marry your wife."

"Which one?" Tree asked.

"The second one."

"That's a relief," said Tree. "I'd kind of like to stay married to my current wife."

11

Freddie was in the shower when Tree got back to the house. He went into the kitchen and phoned the number on the slip of paper Rex had given him. After a couple of rings a voice came on the line and said, "Bonjour. Hello."

"Is this James Devereaux?"

"Yes," Devereaux said. "Who's this calling?"

"My name is Tree Callister, Mr. Devereaux. I'm a private detective down here on Sanibel Island."

"You're kidding," Devereaux said. "I know Sanibel. I would have thought the last thing they need there is a private detective."

"That's what makes it so easy to be a private detective on Sanibel Island," Tree said.

Devereaux laughed and said, "What can I do for you, Mr. Callister?"

"I'm working on something here, and I saw you on television yesterday talking about Vic Trinchera."

"The mob hit down there," Devereaux said.

"Are you certain that's what it is?"

"I don't see how it could be anything else," Devereaux said.

"I guess I was surprised that he was a gangster. I met him briefly, and he didn't exactly come across as Tony Soprano."

"Vic could make Tony Soprano look like a schoolboy," Devereaux said. "I can tell you a little bit about him if it'll help you."

"Sure," Tree said.

"Vic gained notoriety as a young man after thieves broke into the Montreal Museum of Fine Art. Three men used a ladder propped against a back wall to enter through the skylight. The museum was only partially alarmed due to repairs.

The thieves got away with eighteen paintings, including a Rembrandt oil, *Landscape with Cottages*, valued at one million dollars.

"They never recovered any of the stolen paintings," Devereaux continued, "and Vic always denied he had anything to do with the robbery. Yet not long after that, Vic and his brother Sonny were able to acquire a Montreal funeral business. Using the funeral homes he acquired over the next few years as a front, Vic rose in mob circles, as did another young hood, Johnny Bravo, who, it is believed, was also in on the museum heist. You would have thought Vic, the older of the two and more experienced, would have taken over, but in fact it was Johnny who became the crime powerhouse and ran the Montreal Mafia until he was finally convicted on seventeen counts of money laundering and income tax evasion.

"That's when Vic finally had his chance at the big time," Devereaux said. "While Johnny Bravo languished in jail, Vic became boss. He was very good at being bad. At the height of his power, he controlled the construction industry, bribed local and provincial politicians, and killed anyone who got in his way."

"It's hard to believe that little guy in a fisherman's cap ran a Mafia family," Tree said.

"Yes, well, appearances can be deceiving, particularly in the mob world. Vic's reign ended a couple of years ago when Johnny got out of jail and wanted his old job back."

Devereaux explained that Vic fought without success against Johnny's attempts to regain power. By now age was catching up to him. He was facing various health problems, including heart disease and a bout with colon cancer. When his wife and daughter were killed in a car explosion, Vic retreated to Miami, ostensibly so heart specialists could treat him.

"Now he's gone the way most of these guys go—slumped in a car pumped full of bullets. Of course, Vic always maintained he was an honest Montreal businessman who owned funeral homes. He knew nothing about organized crime and protested that he had never been convicted of anything, not even a parking ticket—and that was true enough."

"Did you ever hear anything about a dog?" Tree said.

"A dog?"

"Did Vic have a dog?"

"If he did," Devereaux said. "I never heard about it. What's a dog got to do with anything?"

When Freddie appeared in the kitchen, Clinton marched right over to her and demanded a good ear-rub, which she was glad to provide. Tree poured kibble into Clinton's bowl and told Freddie about his early-morning encounter with Rex. "What did he say?"

"He said he was going to marry my wife."

"Not me, I hope."

"No, I was worried about the same thing. But it's an earlier wife."

"Kelly."

"That's the one." Tree put Clinton's bowl on the floor. The dog abandoned his ear-rub and went over for an exploratory snort of his kibble.

"Do you think that's a good idea?"

"I don't know," Tree said, truthfully. "I have no idea anymore what's a good idea and what isn't. Rex says he's lonely, and he doesn't want to be lonely any longer. Having been lonely in my life, I know how he feels. It's no fun. If Kelly gives him what he needs, I'm happy for him."

"And supposing Kelly doesn't feel the same way about Rex."

"There's not a whole lot I can do about it one way or the other—except support my old friend, and that's what I intend to do."

His cellphone rang. The LCD screen showed it was Edith Goldman.

"I've been trying to get hold of you," Tree said into the phone.

"Where's the dog?" Edith demanded.

Tree tried not to look at Clinton or Freddie when he said, "I told you before, Edith. I don't know what you're talking about."

"Look, Tree, I'm under a lot of pressure here. I have to find that dog. Vic was supposed to hand over a dog. That was the whole point of your meeting."

"The whole point you never bothered to tell me about."

"I'm offering a ten-thousand-dollar reward for the recovery of that dog."

"You're kidding. What's so important about him?"

"Just do this for me, will you, Tree? You're a private detective, find the dog. I'll pay you ten thousand dollars, no questions asked. Just find that dog."

The line went dead.

Freddie gave him *the look*, never a good thing. "Why do I suspect we're in more trouble," she said.

"You're not in trouble," Tree said. "If anyone's in trouble, it's me."

"No," Freddie said vehemently. "That's what you don't seem to understand. You don't get into trouble. *We* get into trouble."

"All I can say right now is that Edith is acting very strange, and I'm not certain why."

"Because her client is dead, and the private detective she hired is lying to her about a certain dog."

"For now, I'm hanging onto Clinton." Tree said.

"He's not your dog."

"His owner is dead, and so for the time being the two of us are all Clinton has. If someone killed Vic Trinchera maybe they want to kill his dog, too. And I'm not going to allow that to happen."

"There is always the traditional way of dealing with this sort of situation," Freddie said.

"That would be the police," Tree said.

"It wouldn't be the first time someone has gone to them," Freddie said. "It has been done before."

"And what do you suppose I would tell them?"

"You would tell them that a Canadian gangster gave you a dog just before he was murdered. Now there are a number of people after said dog."

"Don't forget I've already talked to the police."

"Talking to the Canadian police doesn't count," Freddie said.

"She says it does."

"Not only did you lie to this Canadian so-called police-woman, but I highly doubt she has any jurisdiction here, and therefore is very limited when it comes to providing help."

Tree thought for a moment and then bent down to look at Clinton, now chomping away at his bowl of kibble. He called, "Clinton, come here. That's a boy, come here."

Clinton lifted his head up as though offended anyone should bother him while he was eating.

"What are you doing?" Freddie asked.

"What's the one thing we haven't considered in connection with Clinton?" Tree said.

"I don't think we've actually considered much of anything. So far, all we've had is Tree Callister and his blind determination to hang onto this dog, no matter what."

"I'll tell you what we haven't done. We haven't spent enough time considering why he is so important."

As though on cue, Clinton left his kibble unfinished to stand in front of Freddie and Tree, presenting himself for inspection.

"I mean, Clinton," Tree said to him, "you're a great dog and everything, but what is it about you that makes Canadian Mounties and Montreal gangsters come looking for you?"

"Maybe Clinton knows the secret code to something," Freddie said. "You scratch his ears just the right way, and he barks out the code."

"I wish you could talk to us, Clinton," Tree said, studying the dog closely. "It would be so much simpler if you could just tell us what everyone is looking for."

Clinton turned his head, as if baffled by what these humans were going on about. Tree reached forward and undid the yellow collar Clinton wore around his neck.

"It contains a map to buried treasure," Freddie said.

"You read too many Hardy Boys mysteries," Tree said.

"Not me," Freddie said. "I was strictly Nancy Drew."

The collar was decorated with red metal flowers, slightly raised. He turned the collar over. The printing on the back announced the "original all style, No Stink Collar." It was manufactured by the Dublin Dog Company. Silver studs held the collar's end flap in place and provided anchorage for the buckle and a metal D-ring to which a dog license was attached. It said Clinton was licensed in the city of Montreal. Tree wondered if that made him an outlaw dog here on Captiva.

Tree scraped his fingernail across the license and then tried to pry up one of the flowers. But the scraping revealed nothing and the flowers refused to budge. Clinton had grown bored and lay down.

"Here, let me take a look," Freddie said.

"You're not going to find anything," Tree said, handing her the collar.

"I know, but let me look, anyway."

She turned the collar over in her slim hands. Tree went to the refrigerator and got himself a Diet Coke. Freddie flattened the collar on the counter. She dug a fingernail into the collar's soft undersurface. The edge of her nail caught something and part of the collar peeled away. Beneath the strip of yellow plastic was an address:

O. Crimson
220 NW 26th St.
Miami, Fl.
33127

"You said Vic Trinchera owned Clinton," Freddie said.

"That's what I thought," Tree said.

"Then who is this guy?"

"I have no idea," Tree said.

Freddie said, "Supposing we find out."

"I'm not sure we're going to find anything," Tree said.

"Maybe not, but I haven't been to Miami for a while. We can look up this O. Crimson and then have an early dinner."

"That's what it is," Tree said. "You want to have dinner in Miami."

"Your ability to see right through me is extraordinary," she said with a grin. "Let's get going. I want to Google a couple of restaurants."

12

In the Wynwood district of Miami, the inmates had taken over the asylum. An invading army of artists forever in search of cheap lands to occupy had transformed what had been a maze of warehouses on a rundown industrial wasteland, filling exterior walls with dramatic murals bursting with color, wild pop art creations reminding Tree of the brightly colored Sunday comic pages of his youth.

Two-twenty Northwest Twenty-sixth Street was once a garage. Its entrance was wide open so that Tree and Freddie could walk inside. The interior had been converted into an artist's studio filled with huge canvases.

"Hello," Freddie called. "Anyone here?"

There was no answer. Freddie called again. Tree noted the sign hanging above him on the wall: TODAY IS THE DAY.

Was it? Perhaps it was. But the day for what? He began leafing through the racks of canvases. Crimson's output was nothing if not prodigious, a stew of cityscapes and celebrities, intricate homages to an American culture that always seemed to feature Audrey and Marilyn, Elvis and James Dean. Nothing too daring, Tree decided. Lots of stuff you could safely hang on your living room wall—provided that your wall was the size of a football field.

Tree heard the sound of a motor gearing down. He turned to see a low-slung black and yellow motorcycle turning off the street, slow, and then bump across the threshold into the garage. The bike's rider wore a Daft Punk-style black helmet. A short black skirt allowed the display of long, graceful legs ending in feet incased in ankle-high biker boots.

The rider shut down the bike and eased off, removing her helmet, shaking loose shoulder-length hair. She had the kind of perfectly proportioned features that inspired use of the word beautiful; the kind of face young men with acoustic guitars wrote songs about and remembered wistfully when they grew old.

Tree said, "That's some bike."

The beautiful young woman shook out her long hair again and said, "It's the Ducati Streetfighter. The world's best motorbike, in my estimation, and I have driven them all. Are you a biker?"

"Just an admirer," Tree said.

"We're art lovers," Freddie interjected. "Art lovers with a lot of empty walls to fill."

"Then you have come to the right place," the young woman said. "Please, make yourself at home. The studio is open to everyone. Oliver should be back any time."

"That's Oliver Crimson?" Tree said.

"Crimson, just Crimson." The long-haired young woman removed a velvet bag from the rear of her Ducati Streetfighter and pulled out a pair of high-heel shoes. She proceeded to remove the boots and slip on the heels.

"My name is Shay—Shay Ostler. If I can help you with anything, please let me know."

She drifted off, carrying her biker boots, and disappeared through a door in the rear of the garage. Freddie went back to inspecting the stacks of canvases.

"Any pictures of a dog?" Tree asked.

"Not so far," Freddie said.

Shay reappeared, this time trailing a big, barrel-bellied man springing into view with a flourish that suggested this was opening night for the stage production of his own life. Straw-colored hair was pushed dramatically back in thick waves from a high tanned forehead. "I am here, right now," he called to Freddie and Tree in a deep, sonorous voice. "Where have you been?"

He glided over to take Freddie's hand in two of his. "We share a moment together," he announced looking deep into her eyes. "And that's important. That's all that counts."

Shay announced, "This is *Crimson.*"

Tree half expected a guy in a top hat to appear and snap a whip at a tiger.

"Am I?" Crimson said. "Am I anything that's real? Are any of us? Perhaps we are all just manifestations of our collected desires, hopes, fears, coming together in these semi-fictional characters we call ourselves."

Crimson's head snapped back, as if he needed extra space in which to inspect his visitors. "Tell me where you are from."

"Just up the road on Captiva Island," Tree said.

"Ah, from the real world, then." Crimson sounded disappointed.

"I wouldn't say Captiva is anything like the real world," Freddie said.

"Whatever. Welcome to the unreal world." Crimson punctuated his words with a grandiose sweep of his hand. "This is the world most people ignore. It is the world where every breath you take calls into question the importance of being, where art packs the punch of a Caravaggio painting. This is the world of Crimson, my friends. Stand back, pay attention: art is being made here."

Tree said. "Today, however, we're not so much looking for art."

For the first time, Crimson's sunny demeanor was shadowed by something approaching a frown. "What are you looking for?"

"Answers," Tree said.

Crimson look like someone had clubbed him. "Answers?" he roared. "Don't you know? There are no answers. There are only questions."

Shay came and leaned against him. The heels made her legs seem to go on forever. She towered over Crimson.

"Then we would like to ask you some questions," Freddie said hurriedly, before Crimson could draw the breath that would launch him into his next soliloquy.

"Specifically, we want to ask you about a dog," Tree added.

Crimson's brow curled deep into the dark brown of his skin. "Dog? What dog?"

"A dog named Clinton," Tree said.

Shay looked expectantly at Crimson. The glow of artistic joy had extinguished itself. Crimson's face reformed into a rock wall. "Who are you people?"

"We're trying to find out more about him, about Clinton," Tree said.

"There is nothing to say. I had him. I had many things. Now I don't have those things any longer—the dog included."

"Did a man named Vic Trinchera take the dog?"

"I don't like to hear that name. That name is from the past. I refuse to live in my past—in any past that does not include Audrey Hepburn." Crimson's face clouded over. "I am tired of this. I thought you people might be interesting. But you are not at all. You are doing the worst thing you could possibly do— you are boring me. I want you out of my studio."

A scowl interrupted the perfection of Shay's face. "Don't upset yourself, Oliver."

"I don't get upset, Shay. That's not my style. But these two have brought a bad vibe in with them. Bad vibes are anti-art. Therefore, they must leave before it affects my karma."

"Shame on the two of you," Shay said.

"Yes, it's one of our shortcomings," Freddie agreed. "We have no shame."

Tree placed his card on the nearest trestle table. "If you change your mind and decide you want to talk, give me a call."

The last thing Tree saw as they left was long, languid Shay pressed against Crimson, his face bright with anger.

The sun was lowering, as they came out of the building. The sun caused the three men waiting for them to cast long shadows. The shadows made the trio seem more formidable. Tree recognized them from the Biltmore: the guy with the pockmarked face, on his way to a jazz gig—or maybe just getting back—wearing the same straw hat. Beside him the balding guy looked tired, as though being a grandfather was too much for him. The third, with the mustache and goatee, was Raspy-voice guy.

Why did the men who were about to get you into trouble always look the same? Tree wondered. Somewhere there must be a thug ranch where they graduate these characters. Raspy-voice Guy said to Tree, "There you are, Mr. Callister. How are you, buddy?"

"What is this?" Tree said.

"This is nothing," said Raspy-voice Guy. "Why should it be anything?"

"You're art students, I suppose, out for an afternoon tour of the Wynwood Walls," Tree said.

Pockmarked Guy smiled. "Hey, a comedian. I like that."

Raspy-voice Guy said, "Yeah, we know just the place for your comedy act, buddy. Why don't you come along with us?"

"I don't think we want to go anywhere," Tree said, keeping an eye on Freddie who never took her gaze away from him.

"That's not the right attitude," said Balding Guy.

"Well, we've got to get back to Fort Myers," Freddie said calmly. "You know, beat the rush hour traffic."

No one was actually touching Freddie, Tree noticed. But Balding Guy and the fellow with the straw hat were sticking close enough to ensure that she did not move far. To her credit, Tree thought, she appeared more irritated than scared.

"I don't like this," Freddie said, addressing Pockmarked Guy. "I want the two of you to move away."

"Don't hold it against me, darling," said Pockmarked Guy. "I like to stand beside gorgeous women."

"Did you hear me?" A much sharper tone this time. The two looked at the guy with the raspy voice who appeared to be the leader. He nodded and the others took a couple of steps back from Freddie.

Raspy-voice Guy broke out a reassuring smile. "No one is going to hurt you or your wife, buddy. I'm here delivering a personal invitation from a friend."

"I don't have any friends in Miami," Tree said.

"This is a new friend," said Raspy-voice Guy.

"He likes comedians," said Pockmarked Guy.

"He sure does," said Balding Guy.

"Tell you what," Raspy-voice Guy said to Balding Guy. "Do something that will make our comedian laugh."

"He should be making us laugh," said Balding Guy. "He's the comedian."

"That's okay," said Pockmarked Guy. "Go ahead. Make him laugh."

"I don't think he's going to laugh," said Balding Guy.

"Sure he is," Raspy-voice Guy said.

"Okay," said Balding Guy. He pulled a gun out from under the jacket he wore and pointed it at Tree and Freddie.

"See?" said Balding Guy. "What did I tell you? He's not laughing."

13

Tree, with his lousy sense of direction, had a vague notion the 1968 Chevy Impala they were in was moving southwest along I-95. Their three hosts weren't exactly providing directions, even after Freddie asked for them, as in, "Where do you think you're taking us?"

She sat beside Tree in the rear, clasping his hand, as though that would offer protection from the unknown represented by the three amigos, squeezed into the front seat, facing forward, saying nothing. All Tree could see were bull-like necks straining against collars.

It had grown dark by the time they turned off the highway onto what Tree thought was SW 40th Street. The next thing he saw was the distinctive tower of the Biltmore Hotel looming against the deepening sky.

As soon as the Chevy came to a stop at the front entrance, Pockmarked Guy was out, opening the back door, and then helping Freddie out; a mobster with manners, Tree thought.

The group entered the hotel, scuttling through the lobby and downstairs where there was an arcade leading to the pool area. Marble statues of what appeared to be Greek goddess-like women in flowing robes lined one side of the vast swimming pool, keeping an eye peeled for drowning hotel guests. Freddie looked impressed. "My goodness," she said.

"It was once the largest swimming pool in the world," Tree said.

"Is that a fact?" said Raspy-voice Guy, also impressed.

"Johnny Weismuller used to be the swimming instructor here," Tree said.

Raspy-voice Guy said, "Who's Johnny Weismuller?"

"A gangster generation gap," Freddie said, rolling her eyes.

Raspy-voice Guy looked momentarily confused as they approached a series of cabanas separated by manicured hedges so that their occupants inhabited their very own forest glade, complete with well-appointed furniture.

Tree and Freddie were led to the end cabana. Raspy-voice Guy indicated they should enter. Tree led the way inside. Three lounge chairs were positioned around a teakwood coffee table.

A moment later, a fragile figure with white hair coughed as he stepped into view. In the dim light thrown off by the nearby pool, he looked gaunt and pale. The loose-fitting white shirt and baggy white linen pants helped, but it was the haunted eyes ringed with dark circles that cast him as a dissolute character out of a Tennessee Williams play.

He coughed again before announcing in a thin voice containing the trace of a French accent, "Pardon, monsieur et madame. Apologies for my tardiness. I have a great deal of business to complete here in the Miami area and just could not get away until now."

"Who are you and what do you want with us?" Freddie asked, cutting to the chase.

"Forgive me, madame. I haven't even formally introduced myself. I am Johnny Bravo."

"Is that supposed to mean something to me?" Freddie said.

"And you are Madame Stayner. Fredryka, isn't it? But you haven't taken your husband's last name, have you?"

"What I don't know," Freddie continued, "is why you forced us to come here."

Johnny Bravo's white eyebrows popped up in surprise. "Force you? No one forced you, but I did want to meet you because of your husband's work with my late friend, Vic Trinchera."

"I never worked for him," Tree interjected. "And I suspect he's not your friend."

"Vic and I had our differences, but I owe him a great deal," Johnny said.

"You pulled your first robbery with him, I believe," Tree said.

Johnny considered this and smiled slightly. "That's the legend, isn't it?"

"I understand they never recovered any of the paintings you stole," Tree said

Johnny Bravo studied Tree for a time before he said, "You have been doing your homework, Monsieur Detective. Or did Vic tell you about me?"

"Vic didn't tell me anything," Tree said. "And I am not a detective."

"That's not what I have been led to understand. The Sanibel Sunset Detective Agency, isn't it?"

"I'm retired," Tree said.

"But you may have been the last person to see Vic alive."

"Whoever killed him had that distinction," Tree said.

"You visited Vic's home in Coral Gables, and now you have Vic's dog. Am I right about that?"

"I don't have a dog," Tree said.

"The question I have is this: did Vic hire you to take care of his dog?"

"He didn't hire me, and I don't know anything about a dog," Tree said evenly.

"Don't play coy with me, Monsieur Detective." The smile was gone now. Johnny Bravo didn't look quite so frail in the failing light, his pale face hardening. "I want us to be friends."

"Maybe I have enough friends," Tree said.

"Well, you'll want to add me to your list. Certainly you wouldn't want me for an enemy."

"That sounds like a threat," Tree said.

Before he could answer, Johnny Bravo lurched forward, shoved violently by a figure bursting through the entranceway.

Swiftly, the cabana filled with men in blue windbreakers, the letters FBI emblazoned in big yellow letters, guns drawn, everyone shouting a cacophony of orders to lie on the ground and keep hands where they could be seen.

Down on his stomach, Tree spotted Freddie through a shifting haze of sneaker-clad feet. She was also on her stomach, trying to explain that she and her husband had nothing to do with this, that they did not know who these people were, and that they were innocent bystanders brought here against their will.

Good luck getting anyone to listen to that reasoning, Tree thought. When cops were swarming, hollering unintelligible commands, the adrenalin flowing like molten lava, nobody was listening. Everyone was on edge, wanting orders followed.

Tree's hands were roughly pulled behind his back and a plastic band twisted around his wrists, binding them together. Then he was unceremoniously yanked to his feet. He caught a glimpse of Johnny Bravo, mouth pulled into a painful smirk, arms also bound behind him, surrounded by grim-faced agents. He noticed with relief that they lifted up Freddie, the only woman present, with a great deal more care than they handled the males.

Tree was pushed out of the cabana, hustled around the pool at speed, as though the agents wanted to be out of there before guests realized that a major bust was going down in the midst of the Biltmore's five-star luxury.

14

The suspects were transported to an office building in North Miami Beach. Tree was taken up a freight elevator, pushed along a corridor, and placed in an airless room with white walls. He sat on one of the two chairs positioned on either side of a gray-metal table, his hands still bound. He sat there for three-quarters of an hour before an agent came in carrying a file folder that he placed on the desk.

He said he was Special Agent Max Hesselgesser. He said this as he undid the plastic strips from Tree's wrists. Relief surged though his body as he held out his freed arms.

"That's better isn't it, Walter?" Hesselgesser said, seating himself across from Tree. If the FBI had a Tough Guy Department, Hesselgesser must have been in charge of it. He had a shaved head, a hard, square face, and the sort of muscular build you get when you go to a gym and not the nearest bar after work.

"You are Walter Tremain Callister. Have I got that right?"

"I want to know that my wife is all right," Tree said.

Special Agent Max Hesselgesser looked at Tree for a moment before he said, "The woman we brought in, she's your wife?"

"Correct," Tree said.

The agent consulted the file in front of him. "The two of you don't have the same last name," Max Hesselgesser said.

"Nonetheless, she is my wife and I want to know that she is okay."

"I suppose that depends on what your definition of 'okay' is, doesn't it? If you mean do we have her in the other room beating her with a rubber hose? No, so in that sense she's okay. If you mean are the two of you facing possible criminal charges, then I would have to say neither one of you is okay—unless you start to cooperate with us."

"What sort of criminal charges would we be facing?"

Hesselgesser consulted the file again. "It appears you've got quite a rap sheet going here, Walter."

Rap sheet? Tree never imagined the day would come when anyone would tell him he had an FBI rap sheet. The perils of growing old.

"Major league stuff," Hesselgesser continued. "A couple of murder charges."

"I was cleared of those charges," Tree said.

"So you were, Walter. So you were. But now you've encountered Special Agent Max Hesselgesser, and I'm a pretty tenacious son of a gun, so you may not find this hoop so easy to jump through."

"You still haven't told me what I'm being charged with," Tree said.

"You haven't been charged with anything yet."

"Then why are you holding me?"

"It says here you are a private investigator," Hesselgesser said.

"Retired," Tree said.

"Okay, Walter, what's a retired private eye doing hanging around with a gangster named Johnny Bravo?"

"You still haven't explained why you are holding me, Special Agent."

"I'm holding you, Walter, because I want you to answer my question." A certain tightness had entered Hesselgesser's voice.

"Here's the thing. I don't want to answer your question."

"I think you would be best advised to answer me, Walter." If it was possible, Hesselgesser's face had become harder. The muscles around the corners of his mouth performed little dances of tension.

"Tell me this, Max. Why did you arrest Johnny Bravo in the first place?"

"You've got it all wrong here, Walter," Hesselgesser said. "I ask the questions. You provide the answers."

"Max, with all due respect, if you want me to answer your question, then you had better answer mine—particularly since the answer to my question is probably going to be in the *Miami Herald* tomorrow morning."

Max Hesselgesser drummed his fingers briefly against the surface of the desk before he said, "We're holding Mr. Bravo as a person of interest in a murder investigation."

"The murder of Vic Trinchera?"

Hesselgesser allowed his head to move up and down slightly. "What do you know about it?"

"Not much," Tree said. "I got a call from my lawyer saying someone in Miami wished to speak to a private investigator."

"That was Vic Trinchera?"

"It was," Tree said.

"What did he want?"

"I never found out," Tree said. "When I got to his house, he drove away, and the next thing I knew, the police found his body."

"How did you get hooked up with Johnny Bravo and his pals?"

"My wife and I were at the Wynwood Walls. His people pulled up and said Johnny Bravo wanted to meet with us."

"Why would Johnny Bravo want to meet with you?"

Tree shrugged. "He wanted to know what I was doing with Vic Trinchera."

"What did you tell him?"

"I didn't tell him anything. I didn't have the chance, thanks to you guys."

Hesselgesser spent more time drumming his fingers against the edge of the table. "Vic Trinchera didn't say anything to you about a dog, did he?"

Tree felt everything inside him tense. "Dog?" he said as casually as he could manage.

"Yes, a dog. Did he say anything about a dog?"

"He didn't say much about anything," Tree said.

"No dog?"

"Why would the FBI be interested in Vic Trinchera's dog?" Tree said.

"Maybe the dog's a witness to Mr. Trinchera's murder," Hesselgesser said. It was hard to tell if he was kidding.

"If you're not going to charge me with dognapping, then I'd like to collect my wife and go home," Tree said.

"You want to know what I think, Walter?"

"I don't like being called Walter," Tree said.

"I think you know a whole lot more than you're telling us."

"About what?"

"I don't know. How about dogs and Vic Trinchera's murder?"

"What is it about me that convinces police officers throughout South Florida that I'm involved in various murders."

"Because you probably are, Walter. My experience? Where there is smoke, there is fire." He rapped his knuckles against the table. "From here on in, I'll be keeping a close eye on you."

Hesselgesser slid a business card across the table. "Keep in touch," he said.

"I'm adding you to my Christmas card list," Tree said.

15

By the time they got a taxi back to the Wynwood Walls—the FBI refused to drive them—and retrieved Freddie's Mercedes, it was after eight. Tree was fighting fatigue as he turned the car off North Miami Avenue onto I-95, headed west out of the city. Freddie, on the other hand, positively crackled with energy. Her brush with gangsters and law enforcement, rather than making her miserable and concerned, had left her pumped.

"What did you tell them?" she said to Tree. "Do you suppose our stories matched?"

"I don't know," Tree said. "What was your story?"

"I just told them what was more or less true—that these guys jumped us and drove us to the Biltmore Hotel. The agents interviewing me asked what I knew about this Johnny Bravo. I said I didn't have a clue who he was, that you'd better ask my husband."

"This agent, Max Hesselgesser, asked me about Vic's dog."

"You're kidding. He wanted to know about Clinton? What did you tell him?"

"That I didn't know anything about a dog."

"So you lied to the FBI."

"I wouldn't put it quite that way."

"What other way could you put it?"

"Did they ask you about the dog?"

"Not a word."

They drove in silence for a few minutes, Tree trying to stifle yawns, breathing deeply to keep himself awake.

"Tell me this," Freddie said finally. "Why do we keep lying about the dog?"

"Because we are trying to protect him."

"From the FBI?"

"From everyone until we find out what's going on."

Freddie said, "You know the one person who might have some answers."

"Edith Goldman?"

"Who is also looking for the dog, is she not?"

"She's even offering a reward."

"Maybe it's time we found out why."

"Should I give her a call?"

"No," Freddie said. "You've tried that, and you didn't get anywhere."

"What are you suggesting?"

"Let's not give her a chance to ignore us."

"How do we do that?"

"We drive around to her place," Freddie said.

"Now?"

"It's Sunday night, probably the best time to get her at home. Besides, I have to go to work tomorrow, so if we're going to do this together, we'd better do it now."

Tree gave her a sidelong glance. "I thought you wanted me to retire."

"You are retired," Freddie answered. "You're a *retired* detective trying to help a dog named Clinton."

"It makes so much more sense when you say it," Tree said.

"My logic is impeccable," Freddie agreed.

Edith's townhouse was within walking distance of her office in downtown Fort Myers. It was after eleven by the time Tree found a parking spot on the street. He hobbled out of the car, stretching his sore joints. Freddie, meanwhile, hopped out and was halfway along the block before she realized her husband wasn't with her.

"Come on," she called to him with an impatient wave of her hand.

"I'm too old for this," Tree said.

"No kidding," Freddie said.

She was already up the walkway to the townhouse. A light shone in the ground-floor windows. Freddie rang the doorbell. Chimes sounded from inside.

Tree joined Freddie at the door and together they waited. Freddie rang the bell again. "Could be no one's home," Tree said.

"There are lights on," Freddie said.

She rang the bell a third time and then pounded on the frosted glass. The door swung open a crack.

"That was the door opening," Freddie said.

"Yes." Tree felt his stomach turn. He had experienced this sickening, sinking feeling before, and it was never good.

Freddie pushed the door open wider. Amber light glowed from the interior. "Edith," Freddie called. "It's me. Freddie Stayner. Are you here?"

Tree was hoping against hope Edith's husky voice would come back to them, urging them to come on in, and could she pour Freddie a glass of wine, and what a pleasant surprise, and sit down and let's chat.

But that did not happen. There was only silence.

"I don't like this," Freddie said in a whisper, as though it was necessary to keep their voices low.

Tree stepped through the doorway into the entry hall, calling out, "Edith, it's Freddie and Tree. We're coming in."

The hallway opened into a living room. Ivory walls displayed modern art pieces. Tree moved through the living room, sensing rather than seeing Freddie behind him. He called Edith's name again, stepping down another short hall leading to the kitchen.

The kitchen floor was done in Italian tile. Tree remembered Edith saying that she had picked it out herself during a visit to Positano. A widening crimson pool spread across the tile.

Behind him, Tree heard Freddie draw in her breath sharply. She grabbed at Tree's arm. He held her, and she began to tremble against him, her eyes welling with tears.

Edith Goldman sprawled on the tile. Her coiffed head swam in red.

16

A blur of sirens and flashing lights and uniformed officers, detectives who looked as though they had just come from their sons' softball practice, badges hanging from thin chains around sun-reddened necks, crime-scene techies in white "bunny suits," questions, questions, and more questions—all the questions rising to a scream: what were they doing in Edith's house? How was it they came to find her body?

Good questions. What were they doing, anyway? Why was he finding yet another bloody corpse, surrounded by dour cops? Too many cops. Florida overflowed with cops. It seemed Tree had met them all, and they all looked at him suspiciously, as though every word out of his mouth was a lie. They were more or less right—not every word necessarily, but enough of them to justify the suspicious looks.

The Fort Myers detectives were short on information about Edith. She had been shot three times. Twice in the back of the head. Once in the chest. That's all they would say. Instead, they wanted to know what Tree did for a living. Tree had no choice but to tell them he was a private detective, a retired private detective he hastened to add. But they did not seem to hear the retired part. A private dick had found Edith's body. What was all that about? Did Tree know more than he was willing to confess? They always thought Tree knew more, when in fact he did not know much of anything.

Tree told his interrogators he and Freddie drove to this townhouse after several calls to Edith had gone unreturned. They decided to go to her place to make sure she was all right. Not quite a lie, but not the truth, either. He did not mention, for example—and neither did Freddie— that two hours before they found Edith they had been sitting with their wrists bound answering questions posed by the Miami FBI, questions about a missing dog—a dog everyone appeared to want, a dog that may have gotten Edith Goldman killed. Would you kill someone over a dog? Tree wondered.

Apparently that was a possibility.

It was after one o'clock by the time the police finally released them. Freddie leaned close to Tree, holding his arm as he drove. There were no further tears but occasionally her body shook involuntarily.

They crossed the causeway onto Sanibel in silence and then started along Periwinkle Way. The business of being kidnapped, arrested, questioned, and then discovering a dead body and being questioned more, had left them numb and exhausted.

The island was quiet at this time of night. You could fool yourself into thinking that only the two of you were left in the whole world, stranded in a darkness broken by flashing images of Edith Goldman swimming in blood.

"I don't like this," Freddie said as they crossed Blind Pass onto Captiva. "This isn't fun."

"No," Tree said. "No, it isn't."

"Finding dead bodies, people we know. I mean, Edith. We *know* her. She's been to our house. And there she was, lying murdered on the floor."

"It's why I'm getting out of it," Tree said.

"Except you aren't out of it," Freddie countered.

That unarguable truth reduced him to silence.

"Who could have done it?" Freddie, asking the question asked ever since anyone first bothered to investigate a murder.

"It wasn't Vic Trinchera, because he's dead, and it's not likely Johnny Bravo since the FBI has him in custody."

"I can't believe it. I can't believe any of this," Freddie said.

Tree didn't say anything. He turned the Mercedes onto Andy Rosse Lane and a moment later they were pulling into the drive beside their house.

"Clinton's going to be ready to burst," Freddie said.

"He's probably already peed," Tree said. "I can't imagine he held it in this long."

"Great," Freddie said. "That's really what I feel like doing at this time of night—cleaning up dog pee."

"I'll clean it up if he's done something," Tree said. "And I'll get him out for a walk."

"You're an angel," Freddie said.

Tree got out of the car and Freddie followed him to the door. He put his key in the lock and turned it, anticipating Clinton waiting on the other side of the door with a shoe in his mouth.

Except when he stepped inside, there was no sign of Clinton. He called the dog's name, expecting the scrape of his nails against the hardwood flooring as he hurried to greet them. But there was nothing.

Tree turned on a light and Freddie gasped. The interior of the house had been ransacked.

And Clinton was gone.

———

They debated whether or not to call the police.

"If we call, we have to tell them about the dog," Tree said.

"Yes, we would have to," Freddie agreed.

Tree said, "I don't want to do that."

"You're being irrational," Freddie said. "Someone has taken the dog. Someone broke in here and took the dog."

"I wonder about that," Tree said.

Freddie tried not to look at him as if he was crazy—and failed. "What are you talking about?"

"Someone broke in here, yes, but did they find Clinton?"

"He's not here," Freddie said, trying to be reasonable in front of a husband who was sounding more irrational by the moment. "What makes you think they didn't?"

"I don't know, a feeling, something. He's too smart to be taken away by just anyone."

"Tree, he's a dog—a very gentle dog."

"Let me take a look around the neighborhood before we do anything. Maybe he's hiding out."

"This is crazy," she said. "So much has happened already tonight. And now this. I can't deal with anything else. I need to get some sleep. I've got an eight o'clock meeting, and I'm dead tired."

"You go to bed. I'm going to have a look outside."

"Tree, please."

"I know. You're probably right. If I don't find anything, I'll call the police in the morning."

He went out and stood on Andy Rosse Lane, willing Clinton to appear from the shadows, tail wagging, delighted to see his pal Tree. But the shadows did not move. A warm ocean breeze enveloped him as he began walking toward the beach, trying to think of where Clinton might go if he got away from the intruders, thinking Freddie was right, that this was ridiculous. The dog was gone and Tree Callister, retired private detective, did not have a clue as to how to get him back.

The moon struggled out from behind a cloud bank, illuminating sand, glistening like diamonds. The sound of a rumbling sea came to him out of the blackness. Tree made his way along, calling out Clinton's name. Only the whispering night answered. He came to a stop, hoping Clinton would come dashing out of the darkness—willing him to come.

But he never came.

After an hour or so, Tree, barely able to keep his eyes open, decided to turn around and start back toward Andy Rosse Lane. He tramped away from the shore and reached a low seawall. Maybe he'd sit down a moment and rest. He was so tired—and depressed, and angry with himself for leaving Clinton alone in the first place. If everyone wanted the dog, and thought Tree had him, didn't it make sense that someone might come looking for the animal? He should have thought of that possibility—or at least taken it much more seriously—a whole lot earlier.

He slumped down on the sand, and then propped himself so that his back was against the seawall. Yes, that was much more comfortable. The wind had picked up somewhat, like a warm blanket wrapping itself around him. His eyes fluttered shut.

He dreamed.

Clinton on a sunny morning bounding along the edge of the surf, long spindly legs in awkward synchronization, ears flapping away—the joy of being a dog on a perfect day. And Tree was right there with him, a young man again, bronzed legs pumping hard to keep up. Exhilarating.

Something nuzzled against him. That familiar nuzzle. Tree kept his eyes closed and smiled inwardly. He knew Clinton would come back. All he had to do was believe, and Clinton would be there and everything would be okay.

He opened his eyes.

17

B ut it wasn't Clinton.
The pallid, somber face of Royal Canadian Mounted Police Sergeant Melora Spark loomed over him.

"What are you doing here?" Tree said to her.

"What am I doing here?" She appeared taken aback by the question. "Yes, well, what am I doing here? I could ask you the same question."

Tree raised himself off the rough stone surface of the seawall. A shard of pain shot through his back. He groaned and looked around. Hints of dawn streaked the horizon. The breeze had cooled considerably. A seagull fought against it for a moment and then gave up and darted away.

Melora straightened up as Tree rolled onto his knees. She stepped back as he braced his hand against the top of the seawall and pulled himself to his feet. She took a couple of more steps back, as if anticipating an attack.

"I would like to know what you're doing out here," Melora said.

"What does it look like?"

"It looks like you passed out on the beach."

"I didn't pass out. I dozed off."

"Isn't that a little strange?"

"Is it?" Tree said. "I guess I hadn't thought much about it until you came along. Which reminds me. You still haven't told me what *you* are doing here."

"I told you before. I am investigating the murder of Vic Trinchera."

"The killer is here on the beach?"

"Okay, if you weren't so busy falling asleep on beaches, you would know that you are all over the news this morning."

"Why would I be all over the news?"

"Could it have something to do with the fact that Johnny Bravo was arrested in Miami yesterday and at the same time they picked up you and your wife for questioning?"

"I see," was all Tree could think of to say.

"Now that's Miami. In Fort Myers, your name is on the local news as the person who discovered the body of Vic Trinchera's attorney, a woman named Edith Goldman. Foul play is suspected, according to the police."

"Yes, someone murdered her," Tree said.

"Let's put it this way, Mr. Callister, I find your actions and your movements highly suspicious for someone who is supposedly retired and professes not to be involved."

"I'm not involved," Tree insisted.

"Then what are you doing associating with a known gangster like André Manteau?"

"Who?"

"André Manteau. In Miami, he goes by the name Oliver Crimson."

"He's not a gangster. He's an artist."

That brought a derisive snort. "Just goes to show you what you know. Manteau is no artist. He is well known in Quebec as Le Manteau Noir—the Black Coat—the leader of a motorcycle gang, The Devil's Headsmen."

"Come on," Tree said. "Don't tell me Crimson heads a motorcycle gang."

"He claims he's out of it now," Melora said. "He says he is living quietly in Miami concentrating on his art, but we suspect that he is still very much involved with The Headsmen. They have been feuding with Vic Trinchera and his mob for years."

"What did they feud about?"

"André accused Vic Trinchera of stealing his dog."

Tree said, "The dog you're looking for."

"The dog you are here on the beach trying to find," Melora said.

"I don't know what you're talking about," Tree said.

"Yes, you do," she said.

"Why is everyone so interested in this dog, anyway?"

"Why are you so interested?" she shot back.

Because in a short period of time he had fallen in love with the dog, and believed he was the only one who cared about his safety and well-being? Yes, that was the answer to the question, all right. Except now he had lost the dog, and how was he ever going to find him again with Melora Spark following him around?

Whatever his current confusion of feelings, he did not care to reveal them to a Canadian Mountie, so he shrugged, and said, "I've been dragged into something, thanks to Edith. Every time I try to extract myself, something else happens, and now I'm in deeper. The one thing everyone has in common, they want this dog. So I ask you again, Sergeant, what is it about the dog?"

Melora looked at him a long beat before she said, "I'm afraid nothing has changed, Mr. Callister. I'm still not at liberty to say anything to you about an ongoing investigation. I'm particularly reluctant to say anything to an individual I know is lying."

"I didn't know Crimson was a notorious Canadian biker."

"But you have the dog in your possession. At least you did until you apparently lost him. Now you've been out most of the night looking for him."

When Tree didn't say anything, she added, "If you find the dog, you had better let me know. Whether you want to believe it or not, I can help. Otherwise, you are dealing with dangerous people, Mr. Callister, and you are in a great deal of trouble."

18

The kitchen phone was ringing as Tree entered the house. The readout said it was Freddie calling from work.

"I've got the dog," she said as soon as he picked up.

"You're kidding. Where was he?"

"One of the neighbors found him in her back yard. I was frantic, not knowing what to do. There were all sorts of emergencies at the office. You weren't here, and who knew what had happened to you. I was in a panic. I came out onto the street to look for you when our neighbor appeared dragging along a rather sheepish-looking Clinton."

"I can't tell you how relieved I am," Tree said.

"I know, darling. I've been trying to call you. I didn't want to leave Clinton alone, so I brought him to work with me."

"He's must have gotten out when the house was broken into," Tree said. "He's a smart boy, our Clinton."

"Also very, very lucky," Freddie said. "I'll keep him here today and then bring him home tonight."

"Okay."

"Sorry I couldn't stick around, but Clinton was back and things are crazy here."

"I understand," Tree said. "I love you."

"I love you, and the dog loves you," Freddie said before she hung up.

Feeling much better, Tree stripped off his clothes, shook the sand out, and stepped into the shower. He thought of turning on a television set to hear what CNN was saying about events of the previous night, decided he couldn't face it, and got dressed instead.

He was in the kitchen making coffee when there was a knock at the front door. He groaned inwardly. Was TV news outside with a camera truck and some kid armed with a nice haircut and a microphone?

But it wasn't a newsperson at the door. At least not a local newsperson. It was Kelly Fleming, the ex-wife and former Chicago television newswoman, chic and radiant as usual. No matter what happened to Kelly, no matter what indignities befell her, she would always look the way she looked now, as though someone polished her to perfection a moment before she stepped out in public.

"Are you going to stand there with your mouth hanging open, or are you going to invite me in?" Kelly said.

"I was just making coffee."

"I don't drink coffee," Kelly said as Tree stepped back to allow her inside. "I don't do anything that might speed up my body's state of deterioration."

"So far you seem to be holding up pretty well," Tree said.

"You always were a good liar,"

"Was I?"

"I'll take a glass of water if you have it," Kelly said.

She followed him into the kitchen, saying, "You have a lovely home, Tree."

"It's not me, it's Freddie."

"She seems wonderful," Kelly said. "You are a lucky man."

"Yes, I am." He ran cold water, filled a glass, and handed it to her. "Sure I can't get you anything else?"

"No, this is fine." She leaned against the counter, sipping the water. She wore white shorts and a halter top, her skin smooth and lightly tanned.

"How do you like Sanibel?" Tree asked.

She put the glass on the counter. "Rex keeps at me to go out in his boat."

"Yes," Tree said. "Rex and that boat."

"I don't think he's all that comfortable with it, particularly when it comes to parking."

"Here they call it docking."

"What's he doing with a boat, anyway? There always seems to be something wrong with it."

"It's South Florida. He thinks anyone who lives here must have a boat. And if you do have a boat, you have to deal with the fact that there is always something wrong with it."

"I'm a city girl. I like pavement under my feet."

Tree grinned and said, "After Chicago and the newspaper business, it took me some time to get used to this."

"Except you don't have a boat."

"Rex has one. That's close enough."

"Rex seems very happy here."

"The boat aside, he's in his element," Tree said. "Everyone loves him; everyone wants to hear his old Hollywood stories."

"Yes, those stories," Kelly said. "It seems to me I've heard them before."

"Many times," Tree agreed. "They haven't changed over the years, but the great thing about this island, there's always a new audience."

She gave him one of those sideways looks that always got to men—except Tree, of course. He would never fall for a look like that. Not anymore, anyway.

"Now you, Tree, you don't seem to be bored here; just the opposite, in fact."

"Hey, I'm just a quiet retired guy," Tree said.

"Who happens to be all over the news this morning."

"So I hear."

"You haven't turned on a television or read a newspaper?"

"I haven't had time," Tree said.

"Kidnapped by gangsters in Miami. Discovering dead bodies in Fort Myers—no getting bored for intrepid Tree Callister."

"That's me," Tree said, forcing a grin, not certain where this was going.

Kelly picked up her water glass, took it to the sink, and refilled it under the tap. "You know I was downsized last year."

"I didn't, not until you told me at the Lighthouse."

She turned to him, holding the glass. "It was quite a blow."

"I can imagine," Tree said.

"I'd been part of Chicago television for twenty-five years. Six local Emmy Awards for my work."

"Yes, I remember," Tree said.

"I turned down opportunities in New York because I wanted to stay in Chicago. I love the town, love the news scene there, love being part of it—the craziness, the corruption, the crime, all of it."

"And don't forget all the attention you receive," Tree said. "You love walking into a room and being Kelly Fleming."

"Hey, it comes with the territory," she said with a smile. "I decided a long time ago that I might as well relax and enjoy it."

She drank some more water and then once again put the glass to one side. "The point is, it's over, and I don't like it. I don't like it one bit. I'm about as good at being retired as you are."

"I don't mind being retired," Tree said. "I just don't seem to be able to do it."

"I'll be honest with you. I'm looking for a way back in, something I can take to them that would put me back in the game."

"That sounds like you're planning to leave the island."

She lifted her shoulders up and down and abruptly looked tired. "I don't know. Rex wants me to stay, of course."

"I care about Rex," Tree said. "I don't want to see him hurt."

"Don't worry," Kelly said. "I'm not going to hurt him."

"Then stick around for a while."

The tension went out of her body, and she turned on that smile that previously had charmed the world. "Is that what you would like?"

He didn't say anything. She looked back at him. "I'd better get out of here," she said.

He said, "Without telling me why you came."

"Maybe I'm not all that sure. A little advice about Rex, maybe."

"I'm not quite sure what to say other than it's awkward talking to my former wife about her relationship with my best friend."

"Which is why I should get out of here."

"Do you have a car?"

"Rex is supposed to pick me up at the beach in a few minutes."

"I can drive you back to the Chamber."

"Do you mind?"

They went outside to his car. Tree opened the passenger-side door for her. She went to get in and then stopped. "You know something?"

"What?"

"I can't remember why our marriage broke up."

"I believe you were bored," Tree said.

She gave him another smile. "I think there must have been more to it than that."

"I'm not so sure," Tree said.

And then she kissed him on the mouth.

Just as Rex Baxter drove up in his red Dodge Challenger Hellcat.

19

Rex got out, glanced at Kelly, and then said to Tree, "I heard about Edith Goldman."

"Yes," Tree said.

"I thought I'd drop around and see how you're doing."

"I'm doing okay," Tree said.

"You shouldn't have stopped being a detective," Rex said. "You're in more trouble than ever."

Kelly went over and slipped her arm around Rex's waist. "I was worried about Tree," she said.

"I thought you were going for a run on the beach," Rex said.

"I did. I ran on the beach. Then I came over here."

"Where's the dog?" Rex said to Tree.

Kelly's eyes narrowed. She looked at Tree. "Dog? What dog?"

"Tree has a hound dog," Rex said.

"He's not here," Tree said quickly. "Freddie took him to work this morning."

Rex said, "I'd better be getting to the Chamber. Everybody's yelling and screaming about the website. I don't know. It looks pretty good to me."

"Try to remember, darling, it *is* the twenty-first century," Kelly said.

"Yeah, I'll keep that in mind. What are your plans?"

"I'll go back to your place, get cleaned up, check my e-mail, maybe get some sun."

"Why don't I pick you up for lunch around one?"

"You don't need to, honey. I'm okay on my own."

Tree found it strange to hear his former wife calling his best friend "honey." But then maybe his best friend found it equally strange to drive up and find his new girlfriend kissing his best friend.

When they had both driven off, Tree went back into the house. The phone started ringing. He sat on the sofa staring into space and let it ring. He couldn't bring himself to talk to anyone right now.

———

Freddie got home that evening, dragged along by an excited Clinton. He leapt up on Tree.

He hugged Clinton and congratulated him on being such a smart boy, knowing enough to get away from whoever broke into the house. "Yes, you are," Tree said, holding Clinton. "You are such a good boy, and I missed you."

Clinton nuzzled him in happy agreement.

Tree got him water and then fed him a bowl of kibble. Freddie poured herself a glass of chardonnay.

"The question now is, what do we do with him?" Freddie said.

"I'm not turning him over to anyone."

"Obviously I don't want anything bad to happen to Clinton, but at some point we are going to have to tell the FBI or the police about what's going on. There are simply too many people looking for this dog, and we are not really equipped to protect him."

Tree watched Clinton gobbling his kibble and didn't say anything.

"Tree?" Freddie said. "Are you listening to me?"

"Kelly came to see me," Tree said.

"Is that an attempt to change the subject?"

"This is to tell you my ex-wife showed up at the door in the midst of everything this morning."

"What did she want?"

"I'm not sure."

"Should I be worried?"

"No, of course not."

Tree then told her about what had happened, including the part where Kelly kissed him just as Rex drove up.

"What did Rex say?"

"He didn't say anything."

"That's not good."

"No, I don't think so," Tree said.

"You should have a talk with him."

"And say what? My ex-wife, your new girlfriend, kissed me, I didn't kiss her."

"You could say it was meaningless."

"I guess I could," Tree said.

"Providing it was meaningless."

"For me, it was."

"But you're not so sure about Kelly."

"I don't know what to think."

"Maybe you're making too much out of it."

"I hope so," Tree said. "But I can't help worrying about Rex."

"Rex is an adult," Freddie said. "He should be able to figure this stuff out for himself."

"Except he's lonely and vulnerable—and where Kelly is concerned men don't always think straight."

"Including you?"

"At one time it probably applied to me, yes."

"But not any longer?"

Tree laughed and said, "Now it's you—when I'm around you, I can't think straight."

"So that's what it is," she said. "I wondered."

"Yes, you've driven me crazy."

She came into his arms. "You may be crazy, my love, but I'm not sure how much I had to do with it."

She kissed him. He looked at her in amazement. "It's Monday night, for heaven's sake."

She said, "So? You're used to walking on the wild side, aren't you?"

"I'm a veteran walker on the wild side."

"So prove it."

Somehow they were in their bedroom, entwined. They heard a yelp and turned to see Clinton at the bottom of the bed, those big, sad eyes, imploring. "I'm sorry, Clinton," Freddie said. "This is not something you can be part of."

Clinton responded by taking a couple of steps back and then bounding onto the bed. "Clinton," Tree said in a stern voice, "get off the bed."

Clinton sat on his haunches and turned his head a bit.

"Tree, he has to get off the bed," Freddie said.

Instead, Clinton lay down, burrowing into the covers, hoping he wouldn't be noticed.

"He's had a traumatic day," Tree said. "He doesn't want to be alone."

"Good grief," Freddie said.

He pulled her to him.

Freddie said, "I can't believe we just did that with the dog on the bed."

"He was very quiet," Tree said. "You hardly knew he was here."

By now, Clinton had moved up so that he lay contentedly between them. Freddie reached down and petted his head. Clinton uttered a contented sound and wriggled around so that he was even closer to his pals.

"He loves us," Tree said.

"What are we going to do with him?"

"You keep asking that question."

"And you keep not answering it."

"All we have to do for now is love him," Tree said.

"We don't have any trouble doing that, but then what? I'll remind you again, in case you've forgotten: people are looking for him."

"Actually, I do know what I'm going to do."

"Then, please tell me."

"What I started out to do—find out why everyone is looking for him. If it's something we can turn over to the FBI, then we will do it. After that, we'll keep Clinton, and everything will be fine."

"Everything won't be fine," Freddie said.

"You're too much of a pessimist."

"I'm a realist," Freddie said. "This isn't going to end well."

"Yes, it is," Tree said. "I will make it end well. I will."

He told himself that repeatedly as he drifted off, like Dorothy reciting, "There's no place like home." But he now knew the truth about Dorothy. *The Wizard of Oz* wasn't just about getting home. It was about getting Dorothy's dog, Toto, to safety. Saving Toto. Dorothy wanted to reach home because that is where Toto would be safe.

Tree felt Clinton's warmth against him as he lay back, holding onto Freddie, thinking that, for a moment, all was well with the world. He and Freddie were home, and Clinton was home with them, and they were safe.

20

The next morning Tree drove back to Miami.

The mystery of Clinton was never going to be solved on Captiva Island, he decided. The answer lay to the south.

He told Freddie a white lie—he had errands to run in connection with closing the office. She looked at him dubiously, but nonetheless agreed to take Clinton with her to work.

The drive left him with time to think, always a dangerous state for him. His mind drifted onto the subject of Kelly Fleming and that kiss. From the kiss his mind wandered into irrational territory—the land of idle speculation: what did that kiss mean? The trouble with thinking too much about Kelly, he mused, was that thinking tended to make her motives far too complicated, whereas they were usually pretty straightforward. Kelly cared. Until she didn't care.

When Tree was married to her, he tried to convince himself that there was more to it than that. But he finally concluded there wasn't.

The kiss? That was just a kiss.

He shook off the urge to allow his mind to wander into more dangerously speculative territory. He was happily married. Kelly was a long-ago disappointment—the charismatic news anchor he could not hold onto. Well, age had caught up with her, and although charisma held, she was no longer the popular Chicago newscaster. She was an out-of-work-journalist anxious to cook up something that would get her back in the game.

Was that, then, the reason for the kiss?

Or was the kiss just a kiss?

He arrived at Wynwood early in the afternoon. The sky was unusually overcast as Tree parked the Beetle in an empty space along the street. As he walked around the corner to the garage studio of Oliver Crimson aka André Manteau, the first raindrops began to splatter against the pavement.

The garage appeared deserted. The big entrance door had been pulled down. The blacked-out window panes did not allow anyone to see inside. Along Twenty-sixth Street a wrought iron gate was drawn across a parking area and locked tight below a banner that read DON'T PANIC. Good advice.

Tree returned to the Beetle as the rain came down harder. He got in the car wondering what to do next. He noticed something move in his rearview mirror. He strained around in time to see the gate opening and a red van turn onto the street. Oliver Crimson was behind the wheel.

The van moved through the rain, east on Northwest Twenty-sixth Street. Tree started to follow.

At North Miami Avenue, Crimson turned south, the pelting rain slowing movement. The van turned onto the MacArthur Causeway, choked with traffic, everyone trying to get home. Thus it took forever for Crimson to navigate his van off the causeway. Finally he swung onto Fifth Avenue and then turned south on Ocean Drive where the red van pulled to the curb and stopped.

Tree drove past the van, catching a glimpse of Crimson as he emerged from the driver's side. He found a parking spot and jumped out of the Beetle, ignoring the rain, hurrying back to where the van was parked. He was in time to see Crimson, head down, march across a weedy patch of ground to a flight of stairs running up the side of a nearby building. He climbed the stairs and disappeared inside.

Tree stood in the pouring rain staring up at a sign that read: "For Sale. Vacant Lot and Hotel." The structure, desolate in the rain, was an abandoned white elephant, paint peeling, a ragged chain-link fence strung around its perimeter, making a half-hearted effort to protect the black holes that once had been windows and doorways from unwelcome intruders.

Crossing the weedy courtyard, Tree ducked through an open doorway. Peering into the interior, he could make out a sooty maze of crumbling walls and sagging ceilings. The sound of the thudding rain echoed hollowly.

As he stood there, Tree kept thinking the rain was soon going to let up. This was Florida, where precipitation never lasted longer than it took to wish it would stop. But not today. Today, the minutes ticked past with no sign of Crimson or an end to the rain. His cellphone vibrated in his pocket. Freddie calling. He swiped the phone. "I'm in Miami," he said.

"What are you doing in Miami?"

"Following Oliver Crimson."

A pause before she said, "Why are you doing that?"

"I didn't have a chance to tell you last night. Before he was a Wynwood Walls artist, Crimson apparently was a motorcycle gang leader in Montreal."

"I don't believe it," Freddie said. "Who told you that?"

"My new friend in the Canadian Mounted Police."

"So here's the thing, Tree. You should not be going near this man."

Just then a figure appeared at the top of the steps running up the building on the other side of the courtyard. Crimson, his face bloody, staggered against the railing and then lurched down the steps.

"I'm going to have to call you back," Tree said to Freddie.

"Tree—"

He shoved the phone into his pocket and dashed across the courtyard as Crimson reached the bottom of the stairs and fell to his knees. He clutched a plastic baggie. Tree saw that he was bleeding from his nose and mouth. His left eye was puffy and purple and someone had made a nasty mess of his cheek.

"Are you all right?" Tree asked.

Crimson jerked his head up, surprised to see Tree. "No, you idiot," he yelled. "I'm not all right. I'm bleeding."

He reached his hand up and Tree took it and lifted him to his feet. Crimson dropped the baggie. He groaned. "I need that." He fell to the wet ground, groping around. "Help me up," Crimson ordered, once he had retrieved the plastic bag. "Hurry!"

Tree lifted him up again, and together they started toward the street. "Let's get out of here," Crimson mumbled.

"What happened?" Tree asked.

The question was left hanging because at the top of the stairs, a figure appeared. Crimson screamed angrily and yanked himself away from Tree. Meanwhile, the figure at the top of the stairs fumbled under his jacket.

Crimson, bent down and pulled up his pant leg revealing an ankle holster. With a smoothness that impressed Tree, he drew a snub-nosed revolver from the holster, turned the gun toward the top of the stairs, and fired. The figure jumped in alarm, continuing to fumble. Crimson swore loudly and then fired again. Through the blur of rain, Tree could see the figure at the top of the stairs sag back against the railing. Crimson fired a third shot. The figure jerked sideways and disappeared inside the building.

Crimson, the gun in his hand, turned to face Tree. "Get me out of here," he ordered.

"What are we going to do about that gun?" Tree said.

"We're going to remember I shoot people with it," Crimson said. "Now, help me out."

Tree half carried, half dragged Crimson, holding the baggie against his stomach, onto the street. It was raining even harder now. They got to Tree's Beetle. "What's this?" Crimson demanded.

"It's my car," Tree said.

"This piece of crap?" Crimson's bloody mouth was twisted in disdain. "I'm an important artist."

"You're a guy with a gun, bleeding on a Miami street."

"I'm not getting into this."

"Good," Tree said. "Why don't I just leave you here?"

"All right, all right." Crimson sagged against the car. His face had gone bone white. "What I have to endure," he gasped. "Let's get a move on."

Tree opened the door and lowered Crimson into the passenger seat, then squeezed behind the wheel and started the engine. Next to him, Crimson slumped against the window. For a moment, Tree thought he might have died, but then his eyes flickered a bit, and he looked over at Tree, as if trying to figure out who had rescued him. Then his eyes closed again, and he sank into unconsciousness.

The snub-nosed gun nestled in Crimson's lap on top of the baggie. Tree was tempted to reach over and pluck it away. He moved his hand off the steering wheel. As soon as he did, Crimson's eyes popped open. "Don't even think about it," he said.

Tree put his hand back on the wheel. Crimson settled against the seat and soon drifted off again. The sound of his heavy breathing filled the car, overwhelming the rattle of the pounding rain.

21

Crossing Alligator Alley, Crimson suddenly jerked into consciousness, announcing, "The truth always happens!"

"What?" Tree said.

"Where am I?" Blood caked his cheek and had soaked into his shirt collar. As he struggled to sit up, the gun in his lap fell to the floor of the Beetle.

"We're on Alligator Alley," Tree said.

"Why are we here?"

"I didn't know what else to do with you," Tree said. "I don't know what happened in Miami, but people with guns are after you."

"I need something," Crimson said. He fumbled with the baggie.

With shaking hands he tore open the baggie to scoop out a quantity of white powder. He lifted his finger to his nostril and sharply inhaled. "Ah, yes. That's it. That's better."

"Is that cocaine?" Tree demanded.

"No, you jerk," Crimson said. "It's baking soda. I'm making cookies when I get home."

He inhaled more of the white powder.

"I don't want you using cocaine in my car," Tree said, primmer than he intended.

"You don't, huh? Well, isn't that too bad."

"So what was all that about back there?"

"What is it the newspapers like to say? A drug deal gone wrong? Yeah, that's it. A drug deal gone wrong. They messed with the wrong hombre when they decided to cheat Crimson."

He inhaled more cocaine, his head snapping back each time. Then he glared suspiciously at Tree. "What were you doing there?"

"I happened to be in the neighborhood," was all Tree could think to say.

"That's crap," Crimson snapped. "The truth always happens, man. The truth is you were following me."

"Okay, I was following you," Tree admitted.

Crimson looked as if he could not quite believe what he was hearing. "What's with you, anyway, man? Why would you follow me?"

"For one thing, you're not an artist named Crimson," Tree said, keeping his eyes on the empty road ahead.

"You're right. I'm not *an* artist. I am *the* artist."

"You're a biker from Montreal. Your real name is André Manteau."

"Don't listen to that *crap*, man. Someone has taken fact and twisted it into fiction."

His head rolled against the seat's backrest. He seemed exhausted again. "Life is art, man. Understand that. Anything you do with your life becomes your art. The fiction is turned into your fact."

"So, you are a biker?"

"We all have a past, man. He who has not sinned casts the first stone. Know what I mean? Who filled your head with these lies, anyway?"

"A Canadian Mountie."

Crimson laughed and shook his head. He occupied himself inhaling more of the contents of the baggie. Then he said, "Okay, you've been talking to the Mounties. Listening to their crap. But that still doesn't explain why you were following me."

"I wanted to know more about the dog."

"Dog? Man, what are you talking about? A dog?"

"The French hound you gave to Vic Trinchera."

"You mean the hound Vic *stole* from me."

"I'm trying to figure out why everyone is after this dog," Tree said.

"That's what you're trying to figure out, is it?"

"Can you help me?"

"You know, Tree, or whatever your name is, from what I've seen so far, I don't think you've got the brains to figure any of this out."

"That's why I came back to you, Crimson. So you can help a dumb guy like me. Only I discover you're so smart, you're shooting drug dealers in abandoned hotels in downtown Miami."

Crimson laughed and said, "Our lives crossed like two hot wires."

"What's that supposed to mean?"

Crimson carefully closed the baggie and said, "Pull over to the side of the road."

"We're in the middle of nowhere," Tree said.

"I don't care where we are, pull over!"

"I'm not stopping," Tree said.

Crimson reached down with a pained grunt and grabbed the snub-nosed revolver off the floor. "You are going to pull over or else," he said, pointing the gun at Tree.

"Or else what?"

"Man, how stupid are you? What do you think? Or else I shoot you."

"I'm driving the car, you can't shoot me."

"Don't forget what I told you. Truth, man. It always happens. The truth is, you're living in South Florida, and you're driving with a cocaine addict high as a kite. People like me shoot people like you all the time."

Crimson had a point. Tree eased off the gas and turned the Beetle onto the shoulder and came to a stop. As soon as he did, Crimson jammed the gun into Tree's ribs and said, "Get out."

"Get out? What do you mean get out?"

"Don't make me ask you again. Get out of the car—and leave the keys in the ignition."

"You know I saved your life back there."

"I'm high on drugs. I don't know what I'm doing. Now get out."

Tree lifted the latch on the driver's door and eased himself out. He was stiff from the long drive but felt better when he saw Crimson in even more pain as he slowly extracted himself from the other side. He hobbled around, keeping the gun pointed at Tree, who, realizing what was about to happen said, "Without me, you'd be a dead man."

"Your tough luck that you followed me in the first place. You should have let them kill me."

"I'll keep that in mind the next time."

Crimson chuckled as he opened the driver's side door. "Yeah, well, I don't think there's going to be a next time, my friend."

He was about to get into the car when he stopped and said, "Before I forget. Stay right where you are. I sort of want to shoot you, so one of those wrong moves you hear about, and I will put a bullet in you."

"Gee, thanks," Tree said.

"Here's something for you," Crimson said, almost as an afterthought. "That Mountie you were talking about."

"What about her?"

"Her name is Melora Spark?"

"You know her?"

"Here's a news flash, evidence that the truth always happens: she's no Mountie."

"What is she?"

"More truth, man. That dog?"

"What about the dog?"

"It's not the dog everyone is after."

He got into the car and a moment later, the Beetle sped away.

Leaving Tree standing on the side of the highway. With the rain falling.

———————

Of course, there was no cellphone signal out here, tempting Tree to smash his phone to the pavement in a dramatic show of frustration. But then he thought better of it since such a gesture would be meaningless, anyway. Better to hold the drama and just figure out what to do next.

Let's see, he thought to himself. He was alone on the side of a deserted highway in the middle of Alligator Alley, an area of Florida where they strongly advise you not to end up alone. Faced with those circumstances, someone like him, Sanibel Island's private detective, albeit a supposedly retired private eye, should be able to come up with the next move.

Except he stood there and stood there and couldn't think of anything.

Finally, more from frustration than anything, he stuck out his thumb.

Stupid, really. Who was going to pick up an old guy, soaking wet, slumped along the side of the road with his thumb out in the nowhere of Alligator Alley?

As if to answer the question, two cars flew past in quick succession throwing off sprays of water. Tree barely jumped out of the way in time. Frantic arm waving failed to persuade the cars to stop. His best hope, he decided, was that the state police would happen along, but given his luck so far, just when he needed a cop, none would appear. They showed up only when he didn't want them. They were very good at that.

An eighteen-wheeler crashed past and this time Tree wasn't fast enough and got his pants drenched. He swore loudly at the unfairness of it all, the madness, his stupidity for putting his life on the line for Crimson, a heartless, coke-snorting biker-scumbag who would as soon betray you as breathe. Tree stood helpless in the drizzle, the vast flatness of the landscape all but lost in the mist and the arriving darkness.

22

Luckily, the rain stopped soon after Tree began walking. An hour or so later, he spotted a gas station on the right. A big sign leaning against the side of a slant-roofed, weather-beaten shack said he was approaching Carl's. Live bait was available. Soaked to the skin, but relieved, he hobbled inside. Behind protective Plexiglas, a teenaged girl with henna-colored hair, her broad, bare shoulders tattooed, was busy with her smartphone.

"I'm looking for the restroom," he said.

The girl looked irritated at being distracted. "It's around the side," she said through an opening in the Plexiglas. "You need a key."

She slipped a key attached to a thick piece of wood through the opening. Tree took it, thanked her, and went out the door. He found the restroom and used the key to enter the darkened interior. Immediately, he was hit by a foul smell. He fumbled around until he discovered a light switch.

An overhead fluorescent light produced a curious humming sound before emitting a pale glow that revealed a backed-up toilet surrounded by discarded paper towels. Tree held his breath while he relieved himself. The toilet refused to flush. He swore in exasperation. He tried to wash his hands in the filthy sink, but no water came out of the tap. He swore again. Now he was going to contract some terrible airborne infection from this hellhole restroom and die a terrible death in a nowhere patch of South Florida.

He limped back into the gas station. The teenager with the henna-colored hair held her smartphone in front of her like a mirror—or maybe a pathway to the future.

"Excuse me." Tree slipped the key back through the Plexiglas opening. The teenager continued to study the smartphone screen as though it contained the secrets of the universe. Maybe it did. "I'm kind of stranded out here, and my cellphone isn't working. I'm wondering if you have a phone I could use so I could call for some help."

The teenager regarded him with disinterested eyes. "The telephone is not for customer use," she said by rote, as if she had had to repeat it a million times.

"I understand that," Tree said. "But I'm in a bit of a jam here. I wonder if you could make an exception just this once."

"Can't help you," the teenager said. She went back to her smartphone.

Tree forced himself to tamp down bubbling anger. He took a deep breath and then brought out his wallet. "I'll pay you for the use of the phone."

The teenager looked at him. He slid a twenty-dollar bill through the Plexiglas opening. She gave it a lazy look.

"You got another one of those?"

"No."

She went back to her screen.

"Come on," he said. "Give me a break, will you?"

She looked up from her phone and now there was a spark of anger in those dull eyes. "If you don't quit bothering me, I'll call the cops."

"Yeah, do that, will you? Call the police."

Her eyes looked even angrier. "What a jerk," she said. But she snapped up the twenty, and then got up from her chair, an overweight teen moving slowly to where a phone sat on its cradle. She picked it up and then moved heavily back to the Plexiglas and shoved the phone through. "Make it quick," she said. "I could get in a lot of trouble for this."

Tree picked up the phone and dialed a number. A voice said, "Hello?"

"Kelly?" Not who Tree wanted.

"Hi, Tree," she said. "If you're looking for Rex, he's not here."

"Do you know when he'll be back?"

"No idea. He's gone off to a meeting with someone on the Fort Myers city council."

"Okay, listen. Do you have access to a car?"

"Rex left me his car."

"I need a ride."

"You want me to come and get you?" There was disbelief in Kelly's voice.

"Can you do that?"

She paused and then said, "Where are you?"

23

Tree bought a plastic bottle of Diet Coke. He hated Diet Coke in plastic bottles, but that was all that was available in the glass-fronted cooling unit. He also purchased Rice Krispies Treats from the teenage girl with the hennaed hair. Their fight over the telephone and the extortion of twenty dollars had not improved her disposition.

He didn't want to stay inside with her alternately shooting glares at her smartphone screen and at him. He went out and stood beside the Live Bait sign. He sipped at the Diet Coke and munched on a Rice Krispies Treat. The sun had re-emerged, baking the flat landscape around the gas station, heating the asphalt surface of the highway, so that as the odd truck roared by, its tires sizzled. None of the trucks stopped. Maybe the word had spread about the miserable teenaged girl with the hennaed hair and smartphone fixation.

Tree finished his Coke and Rice Krispies Treats. He paced around outside for the better part of the next hour and a half. Eventually, he gathered the courage once again to face his teenage nemesis and went back inside. She was still engaged with her smartphone and barely glanced at him as he entered. He walked to the back where the glass-fronted refrigerator units contained bottles of water.

He grabbed a bottle and was headed back to the front when the entrance door opened and Kelly stepped inside. "Like old times," she said when she saw him.

"Is it?"

"Me having to come and pick you up from the most unlikely places. The only difference is, now you're sober. You are sober, aren't you, Tree?"

"I am, although I'm considering returning to a life of drink."

In her fetching short shorts and sheer white top, her make-up perfectly applied, Kelly was, as usual, ready for the photo shoot that would never occur out here on Alligator Alley.

She followed him to the counter where the teen monster with the hennaed hair lay in wait in her Plexiglas lair. The teenager glanced up from her smartphone. And then her eyes widened, and her mouth dropped open. She gasped: "Are you Kelly Fleming?"

Tree looked around at Kelly. She smiled brightly at the teenager. "I'm Kelly," she said. "How are you?"

"Wow," the teenager exclaimed. She was off her perch behind the Plexiglas. "We just moved here a year ago. But I grew up in Chicago watching you on the news. You're, like, *famous*. What are you doing here?"

"Just picking up a friend," Kelly said.

The teenager looked horrified. "You're with *him*?" As though that was beyond the realm of possibility.

"I'm afraid so," Kelly said.

The teenager looked as though she would forgive Kelly anything—even the ultimate transgression of being associated with Tree. She waddled out from her fortress behind the counter to where Kelly stood.

"Could I, like, get your autograph?" She handed Kelly a scrap of paper.

"It would be my pleasure." Kelly took the paper over to the counter.

"If you could make it out to Charlene."

As if by magic, Kelly produced a Sharpie. "Are you Charlene?"

Charlene's ear-to-ear grin removed any traces of the teen monster. "It's such an honor to meet you."

"It's great to meet you, Charlene, and thanks for putting up with my friend," Kelly said. She made a deep, swirling masterpiece out of her signature. She presented it to Charlene. "How much do we owe you for the water?"

"Oh, no. It's okay. Take the water. Please."

"You're very sweet," Kelly said. She kissed the teenager's cheek. "Thanks so much, Charlene."

Charlene looked as though she had died and gone to heaven.

"Can you believe this car?" Kelly looked pleased with herself as she gripped the sport steering wheel and swung the Dodge Charger Hellcat onto the highway.

"It's not a car," Tree said. "It's a Hellcat."

"Whatever made Rex buy this thing?"

"He still thinks of himself as a hellcat."

"That kid back there, I'm amazed she recognized me."

"What can I tell you, Kelly?" he said. "You still know how to dazzle, even in the middle of nowhere."

"A lot of good it does me." But her face was aglow.

The car roared down the highway, the sound of the V-8 engine a deep, authoritative rumble. The soul of a certain kind of American manhood called out from under that hood; the muscular assertion that you could still be a real man, if only from behind the wheel of a Hellcat.

Or a real woman—Kelly looked as though she was thoroughly enjoying herself controlling this powerful car. Of course, Tree mused, Kelly enjoyed herself whenever she was in control, whether it was cars or men.

She gave Tree a sideways glance. "Not that I want to pry into your personal life. But do you mind if I ask how you managed to end up out here without a car?"

"Someone stole my car," Tree said.

"That battered old Volkswagen you drive around? Who would want to steal that?"

"A particularly low class of criminal in South Florida."

"What made you call me?"

"I didn't call you, I called Rex."

"But why not Freddie?"

"Freddie is trying to run a business," he said. "I didn't want to drag her away because of my stupidity."

"Is that what it is, your stupidity?"

"Let's just say there are days when I do wonder about the state of my sanity," he said.

"But you're onto something, aren't you, Tree?"

"I'm not sure what you mean."

"Come on, something's going down."

"I was in Miami. My car was stolen when I stopped at that gas station. No more complicated than that."

She threw him another glance. "Then why didn't you call the police?"

"Who says I didn't?"

"If you had, they would have been back there at the gas station, and you wouldn't have needed me."

Tree didn't say anything. They drove in silence for a few minutes. Then Kelly said, "You know when I was talking to you about getting back into television?"

"Yes," he said, striking a tentative note because he was never quite sure what Kelly had in mind.

"I was thinking on the way here that you might be able to help me out."

Tree looked dubious. "Me? What can I do?"

"I think I've still got some juice left in me. Every time I think I don't, I run into someone like that kid back there."

"They still know who you are, Kelly, that's for sure," he said.

"I can work that to my advantage—as long as I have the right story. There is a great deal of interest in you in Chicago, thanks to that young reporter who's been writing about you."

"You mean Tommy Dobbs."

She nodded. "Tommy has turned you into a bit of a local celebrity. I'd like to do something on television with you, in connection with the recent events that put you back on the front page. The two of us packaged with a great story. I believe it's a combination WBBM won't be able to resist."

"Kelly, I don't know what's going on myself. Even if I wanted to do what you suggest, I wouldn't know what to tell you."

"I just picked you up off the side of the road looking like a drowned rat. This is not the life of a quietly retired Chicago newspaperman. You're involved in something, and whatever it is, I want to be part of it."

"You've got the wrong idea about me," Tree said.

Kelly tried to keep the irritation off her face—the irritation Tree had seen many times during their marriage when she wasn't getting her way.

"You know what, Tree? I've been accused of many things, but getting the wrong idea about you is not one of them. I could always see right through you."

She took a deep breath before continuing. "Just so you know, I've already talked to Jim Wetherall at WBBM. They're interested. They want an outline of how I plan to approach the story. All I need from you is your agreement to do this."

"But do what, Kelly?" It was Tree's turn to show exasperation. "You may think you know me, but right now, there's nothing."

"I want to stay here, Tree. I really do. But I can't be sitting around doing nothing. I've got to find something."

"So what you're saying is that if I agree to a story, you'll stick around?"

"I'm saying there would be a reason to stay," she said.

"What about Rex? Isn't he reason enough?"

"Put it this way, he's a reason, but not enough of a reason."

Tree swallowed his rising anger over her attitude and said, "I don't even know if there is a story."

"There's always a story," Kelly said with confidence, a quality she never lacked.

"Let me ask you something," Tree said. "That kiss the other day. What was that all about?"

"We used to be married, Tree. We used to kiss."

"But we're not married anymore."

"I forgot myself for a moment, that's all." She shifted those long legs around and gave him a knowing look. "Would you like me to pull over so I can forget myself again?"

"Kelly," he said, alarmed. "Keep driving."

"Have it your way," she said. "Do we have an arrangement or not?"

"Arrangement?"

"Arrangement. A deal."

"About kissing?"

"About the story."

"Okay, if this turns out to be something, you can have it, for what it's worth," Tree said. "I don't believe anyone in Chicago is all that interested, but if it helps you, fine."

Kelly kept her eyes on the road ahead. But she smiled. Tree saw that smile many times when they were married. A Cheshire cat smile. Kelly the Cat.

Victorious.

24

It was late in the day by the time Kelly dropped Tree at the house on Andy Rosse Lane. This time she did not try to kiss him. But she did give him one more of her Cheshire cat victory smiles, and reminded him that they had "an arrangement," and he must keep in touch.

Tree gritted his teeth. He would have been wiser to call Freddie. He would have been wiser to do so many things.

As soon as he walked in the front door, it was apparent that neither Freddie nor Clinton was there, but that someone once again had been in the house and torn the place apart. Furniture had been upended, pictures stripped off the walls. In the master bedroom, the mattress had been lifted off the bedframe and thrown onto the floor. The contents of the dresser drawers were scattered across the room. Freddie's closets had been examined with a vengeance. His tiny closet with its meager wardrobe was untouched.

As he stood there worrying about what had happened to Freddie and the dog, the phone on the bedside table rang. The LCD readout showed that it was Freddie. Tree picked up the receiver. "Where are you?" he said.

"I'm at the office with Clinton," Freddie said. "I came home with him, saw what someone had done to the house, and got out of there."

"This can't be happening again," Tree said.

"Well, it is," Freddie said. "I've been trying to reach you."

"My cellphone is dead," Tree said.

"Are you all right?" Freddie said.

"More or less," Tree said.

"You'd better come here," Freddie said.

"I can't," Tree said.

"Why not?"

"Someone stole my car."

"Why would anyone steal the Beetle?"

"It's a long story," Tree said.

"It always is." Freddie issued a sigh. "I don't want to leave Clinton here alone, and I don't think it's safe for any of us in the house right now."

"I'll meet you at the corner in half an hour," Tree said. "That'll give me a chance to change into some dry clothes."

"What are you doing in wet clothes?"

"Part of the long story," Tree said.

After Freddie hung up, Tree stripped off his damp clothes, showered, and began to feel slightly more human as he toweled himself off. He had just finished dressing in a clean pair of jeans and a T-shirt when there was a knock on the front door. It was at moments like these, he thought, that he wished he had a gun.

Or maybe it was better at moments like these that he didn't have a gun.

Another knock, much more authoritative this time. When he opened the door, Detective Cee Jay Boone said, "Good evening, Tree. How have you been?"

With her was another detective, Owen Markfield. Tree groaned inwardly. These were the two people he least wanted to see right now.

"The cream of the Sanibel Island police department right here on my doorstep," Tree said, putting on his best game face.

"You have a few minutes to talk to us, Tree?" Cee Jay said this in a way that did not leave a whole lot of choice. A handsome African-American woman, she had lost considerable weight since the last time he had seen her—the newly trimmed Cee Jay, lean and mean and ready to give Tree more trouble.

They had a complicated history together, beginning with her attempt to kill him. She denied the attempted murder charge, and in fact the court had thrown out the case against her. Since then, perhaps out of some deep-seated sense of remorse, she had arranged to help him out on a few cases. But she had also arrested him on more than one occasion. Thus he was never sure at any given time whether she was going to be an ally or an enemy.

"I was just on my way out," Tree said.

"We won't take long, Callister." Owen Markfield, he of the youthfully smooth, sun-burnished skin, the perfectly coiffed blond hair, the expensive aftershave—Owen Markfield was another matter, entirely. He most definitely fell into the enemy category, loudly vowing to destroy Tree in retaliation for perceived past criminal acts. Nothing to those acts, of course.

To *most* of those acts.

So far Markfield had failed in his quest for vengeance.

So far.

"Come in," Tree said, stepping back to allow the two detectives to enter.

When Cee Jay saw the look of the place, she came to a stop and turned to Tree. "Are you renovating?"

"We're in the process of making some changes," was the way Tree framed the lie. Right now, he did not want to deal with a B and E investigation that would only raise more questions than he had the inclination to answer.

"It looks like someone broke in," Markfield said.

"What can I do for the two of you?" Tree said.

"The Fort Myers police have asked us to assist them with an ongoing murder investigation," Markfield said, producing the notebook he always seemed to have on hand when he encountered Tree.

"The investigation of whose murder?" Tree asked.

"Come on, Callister, don't start out like this." Markfield already sounded fed up, and he was barely in the door. "You know damned well whose murder we are talking about."

"It's Edith Goldman, Tree," Cee Jay interjected gently.

"I'm afraid there's not much I can help you with," Tree said. If Owen Markfield was already irritated, Tree thought, it might have something to do with the fact that, as usual when he was around, Tree barely opened his mouth before the lies began to tumble out.

"You found her body," Cee Jay said.

"So you know that my wife and I both gave statements to the Fort Myers police."

"Your name is also on her calendar," Markfield interjected. "She had you down for a meeting the day before she died. Also, you are listed on her phone log a few days before that."

"Yes, like I told the Fort Myers police, we talked about a possible assignment."

"What kind of assignment?" Markfield asked.

"No idea," Tree said. "We never got that far."

"Why not?" Markfield, demanding.

"Because I told her I was retired, that I wasn't taking on any more clients."

Markfield looked at him, failing to hide his surprise. "You retired?"

"That's right," Tree said.

Markfield snorted derisively and made a notation in his notebook. Cee Jay said, "When did this retirement happen?" She too sounded dubious.

"I recently moved out of my office at the Chamber of Commerce," Tree said, a statement that at least approached the truth.

"It appears Edith was mixed up with some pretty unsavory characters," Markfield said.

"Well, she was a criminal defense lawyer in Lee County," Tree said. "I don't suppose she was getting a lot of calls from Harvard Business School graduates."

"We believe that one of her clients was a Montreal, Canada, gangster by the name of Vic Trinchera," Cee Jay said. "Does that name mean anything to you?"

Tree managed to look her straight in the eye when he said, "Why should it?"

"Shortly before Ms. Goldman's death, Vic Trinchera was murdered in Miami."

Tree didn't say anything.

"In her calendar, Edith Goldman penciled Trinchera's name beside yours." Markfield had picked up the thread of the conversation.

Tree made a show of looking confused. "I don't know what to say about that."

"You could say something like, 'I find that peculiar,'" Cee Jay said.

"Okay. I find it peculiar."

"You are certain you don't know this guy," Markfield said.

"I know who he is now," Tree said, skirting an outright lie.

"So you do know who he is."

"His death was all over the news," Tree said.

"There's also something else," Cee Jay said.

"Yes?"

"We received a report of an abandoned car in Coral Gables."

Tree didn't say anything, but the muscles in his stomach began to tighten.

"A 1980 Volkswagen Beetle," she continued.

"Registered to you, Callister," Markfield said.

"Yes, as a matter of fact my car was stolen in Miami earlier today."

"So then why didn't you report it stolen?" Cee Jay said.

"I guess I didn't have the time," Tree said.

Markfield jerked his head up from his notebook. "Your car was stolen, and you didn't have time to report it?"

"I'm having trouble getting my head around why two detectives on Sanibel Island would be so interested in a banged-up old Volkswagen stolen in Miami," Tree said.

Markfield issued one of the smirks Tree had come to recognize as a prelude to trouble. "Exactly. Why would two busy detectives like us ever be interested in a rusted-out old Volkswagen in Miami? Can you explain that?"

"I'm the one who's asking, Detective."

"Maybe it has something to do with the fact that there was a body in your car, Tree," Cee Jay said.

Markfield shot Cee Jay a dark look that suggested his punchline had been robbed from him. Then he addressed Tree. "Do you know anything about that?"

"Whose body did they find?"

Markfield's eyebrows shot up in amazement. "What? Depending on whose body it is you might know something about it?"

"I don't know anything about a body," Tree said.

Cee Jay said, "The Miami police have identified the dead man as a local artist named Crimson, although they say his real name is André Manteau."

25

Freddie chose that moment to come through the front door. She reacted with surprise when she saw the two detectives. "Like old times," she managed to say.

"Yes," said Markfield. "Complete with us asking Tree about dead bodies."

Freddie looked even more amazed. "What dead bodies?"

"There's only one," Tree said.

"Actually, there are two," Cee Jay said.

"So far," Markfield amended.

"Let's be fair," Cee Jay said. "Only one body was found in Tree's Volkswagen."

"The car was stolen," Tree said, speaking to Freddie as much as anyone. "I have no idea how the body got there."

"But you know who Crimson is," Cee Jay said.

Before Tree could indicate she shouldn't say anything, Freddie blurted, "Crimson's dead?"

"So you do know him," Markfield shot back.

"I know his work," Freddie said with impressive speed.

"Then it would just be coincidence that he ended up dead in your husband's Volkswagen."

"I just arrived home from work, so I've got some catching up to do here," Freddie said.

Cee Jay addressed Tree. "This André Manteau in addition to his pursuit of art, was also president of a Montreal-based biker gang."

"Is that a fact?" Tree said.

"This is all very interesting," Freddie said. "But it's late, and I've had a long day, and I'm not very interested in hearing about dead Montreal bikers."

"Even if that biker's body was found in your husband's car?" Cee Jay said.

"Whatever it is, we can talk about this in the morning," Freddie said.

Markfield addressed Tree, giving him a hard look. "So you know nothing about this, is that what you're saying?"

"Freddie's right. It is late. Let's talk about this when I've had a chance to gather my wits," Tree said.

"You mean as soon as you come up with another set of lies to explain how you're involved with yet another dead body," Markfield said. He was having a hard time keeping the anger out of his voice.

Cee Jay turned to Freddie, presenting herself as the voice of reason: "Ms. Stayner, obviously something's going on here. Someone has broken into your house. A dead body has shown up in your husband's stolen car. You're probably in some sort of danger. The police can help, but only if we know what's going on."

"You'll forgive me, Cee Jay, if I don't look at you or Detective Markfield and see two people particularly interested in being helpful," said Freddie.

"Have it your way," Cee Jay said.

———

When the two detectives were gone, Tree turned to Freddie and said, "Where's Clinton?"

"I'm going to take you to him," Freddie said. "I don't think it's a good idea to stay here, seeing as how someone has now broken in twice."

"Where are we going?"

"Never mind that. Just get packed—and tell me what's going on."

"Are you sure you want to know?"

"Only so I won't be quite so surprised the next time the police show up at the door."

As quickly as he could, Tree told Freddie about the day's chaotic events: the drive to Miami to see Crimson aka André Manteau; following him into downtown Miami to an abandoned hotel; the attempt on his life; Tree driving Crimson across Alligator Alley only to be abandoned on the side of the road.

"How did you get home?"

"Kelly drove me." Tree tried to make it sound like this was the most natural thing in the world.

Freddie looked at him. "Kelly Fleming drove out to Alligator Alley and picked you up off the side of the highway?"

"I was trying to get hold of Rex," Tree said.

"Why didn't you call me?"

"Because I didn't want to bother you at work."

"Tree, when you are in trouble, it's okay to bother me at work."

"I'll keep that in mind in the future," he said.

"Good grief," Freddie said.

In silence, they collected toiletries and a change of clothing and stuffed everything into an overnight bag—actually, Freddie *neatly* folded business clothes into a sleek Louis Vuitton overnight bag.

When the packing was finished, Tree said, "You still haven't told me where we are going."

"We're hiding out," Freddie said.

"Where are we doing that?"

"When you're on the run, you don't answer questions like that," Freddie said.

"Are we on the run?"

"Tramps like us," replied Freddie, "baby, we were born to run."

26

They weren't running all that far, as it turned out.

About ten minutes off the island to Gulf Harbor, the gated community on the Caloosahatchee River where Rex Baxter was now keeping his boat, the *Former Actor Too*. They were expecting the fugitives at the gatehouse entrance, thus Freddie was able to drive straight into the vast enclave.

They drove along a brick roadway divided by an island containing carefully tended shrubbery, into a parking lot adjacent to the main clubhouse. Freddie turned off the motor and ordered Tree to bring along their overnight bags. Together, they made their way past darkened tennis courts, down to the docks. Pleasure craft that never seemed to move huddled beneath tarps, ghost boats bathed in moonlight. The *Former Actor Too*, Rex's sleek thirty-two-foot Cobalt, was a replacement for *Former Actor*, the craft that had blown up off Useppa Island. It was berthed in one of the end slips, outlined in soft light.

Rex was on the rear deck holding a beer. Kelly Fleming worked up a welcoming smile from her perch on the stern boat seat. Next to her, Clinton leapt up, gave himself a good shake, and then started his tail flailing away as Tree came aboard. He jumped happily up on Tree, and Tree rubbed his ears, relieved to see him.

Rex said, "You don't get this emotional over me."

"You don't jump up on me every time I walk in the door," Tree said.

"If I had any brains, I'd run the other way," Rex said.

"We really appreciate you looking after him for a couple of hours," Freddie said.

Kelly watched closely as Tree embraced the eager Clinton. He could imagine her trying to gauge what importance the dog might have to the story she hoped was her ticket back into the Chicago television market. If only she knew, Tree thought. Or more to the point: if only *he* knew.

"Would you like something to drink?" Rex said.

"No, thanks," Tree said.

Rex said, "I wasn't talking to you. Freddie, how about it, would you like a glass of wine?"

"I could use one," Freddie said.

"Coming right up," Rex said. He ducked below deck.

"Tell me what's happening." Kelly studied the two of them with a gleam in her eye that Tree knew only too well—Kelly's ambition unleashed.

"Thank you for retrieving my stranded husband this afternoon," Freddie said.

"I've had occasion to pick Tree off the side of the road before," Kelly said.

"As I told you, Kelly. Someone stole my car."

"Is that why the two of you are staying on the boat?"

"Our house was broken into earlier," Freddie said. "The place is a mess. Neither one of us feels like staying there. I phoned Rex, and he was kind enough to offer the *Former Actor Too.*"

"Hey, this is the third-safest community in the United States." Rex was in Chamber of Commerce-booster mode as he returned with Freddie's wine. "If we can ever persuade Tree to move off the island, it's certain to become the very safest."

By now Tree had seated himself with Clinton nestled beside him, his head on Tree's lap. Tree stroked his ears while Kelly watched, eyes agleam with suspicion.

"I don't know," she said. "There's something going on here that I'm missing."

"With Tree, I've discovered, it's just as well not to ask too many questions," Rex said.

"You sure the two of you aren't in trouble?" Kelly said. "Maybe you should talk about it."

"We're fine," Freddie said smoothly. "Right now what we need is a good night's sleep."

"Make yourselves comfortable here for as long as you like," Rex said. "There are fresh towels down below and fresh sheets on the bed, so you should be fine, at least for tonight."

"We really appreciate this, Rex," Tree said.

"Come on, Kelly, let's get out of here, and let these people get some rest." He pointed a finger at Tree. "And you stay out of trouble."

"I'm retired, remember?"

"I'm trying to keep that in mind," Rex said. "However, you're not making it easy."

Kelly was on her feet smiling down at Tree, the glitter still in her eyes. "You'll never retire, Tree."

"You don't think so?"

She shook her head. "You're capable of many things, but I don't think retirement is among them."

"When we were married I used to think sometimes that when you were talking about me, you weren't talking about me at all."

"Who was I talking about?" Kelly asked.

"You were talking about yourself."

Kelly produced another icy smile and said, "I have no idea what you're talking about."

"Can I be honest with you?" Freddie said as they walked Clinton along the moonlit strip of beach that ran through the spit of land beyond the Gulf Harbor boat docks. The moonlight tipped the lapping waters of the Caloosahatchee. The scene called for Dorothy Lamour in a sarong with a ukulele.

"You certainly can," Tree said. "After all, we are married."

"I'm not certain I like your ex-wife."

"You're not seeing Kelly at her best," Tree said.

"No?"

"She's fighting for her professional life, and she thinks I can help her."

"What are you supposed to do?"

"She has this idea that I'm her ticket back to Chicago television. Except she thinks I'm holding out on her."

"You are holding out on her."

"It's like I keep telling her, I'm as mystified about what's going on as anyone."

"That still doesn't explain why I don't like her."

"Maybe it's because she kissed me."

"Or it might have something to do with the fact that you called her for help this afternoon, not me."

"I don't believe it. You're not actually jealous of Kelly are you?"

"It's not jealousy so much as just not liking what's happening to us lately."

"We'll be fine," Tree said.

"Will we? I'm not so sure. Let's recap what happened today. You were involved in a shootout in Miami. Your car was stolen. You were left stranded in the middle of nowhere. Oh, and by the way, someone broke into our house—twice. Let me see, did I leave anything out?"

"You forgot the dead body in the car."

"Of course," Freddie said ruefully. "Silly me. How could I forget a dead body in your car?"

Clinton led them up from the beach and along an adjacent pathway illuminated at intervals by overhead lamps.

Freddie continued: "Now we can add Crimson to the number of people looking for Clinton who have ended up dead."

"Crimson wasn't actually looking for Clinton," Tree said.

"Well, he's still dead. I have this awful suspicion time is running out."

"You shouldn't say that," Tree said.

"Say what?"

"'Time is running out.' It sounds like one of those pulp thrillers I used to read as a kid."

"Consider this, Tree. Maybe your life *is* one of those pulp thrillers you used to read as a kid."

———

The bed in the below-deck cabin was surprisingly comfortable. With Freddie on one side of him and Clinton on the other, the soft lap of the waves against the hull of the *Former Actor Too*, Tree felt more relaxed than he had in a long time.

"Nice," he said.

"You love this," Freddie said. "The man with his dog."

"And his sexy wife," Tree said, cuddling against her.

"Now don't get any ideas, not with the dog here."

"Perish the thought."

"I mean we did this once before. But no more."

"No."

"Not again."

"Of course not."

"Tree," Freddie said. "Good grief. Tree, oh . . ."

27

Freddie was up first thing the next morning, deciding she wasn't going to get properly dressed until she got to her office.

"I can't face this cramped little bathroom," she said, once she had dressed in the previous night's uniform of T-shirt and shorts. "Except when they see me come into the store like this, they're going to think I was out sleeping around."

"Which you were," Tree said.

"When you're doing it with your husband, it's not sleeping around," Freddie said.

"I stand corrected," Tree said.

"What about you? I'm leaving you stranded here with Clinton. What are you going to do, my love?"

"I'm going to do something. I'm not exactly sure what it is just yet."

"You should have a goal," Freddie said. "That's what I tell everyone at work. There should be an endgame that sets you up for success, and provides the outcome you desire."

"Good advice," Tree said.

"So then tell me, what is your goal?"

"To retire so I can keep you happy."

"Tree, I'm serious. We're hiding out on a boat with a dog, and we aren't even certain why we're doing it."

"We are trying to keep this guy safe," Tree said, pointing to Clinton who had returned to his favorite place on the rear deck seat and now watched them with a slightly quizzical expression, not sure what these humans were up to this morning.

"But how long does that go on?"

"I don't know. What do you want me to do, Freddie?"

"Consider turning Clinton over to the authorities. They will keep him safe."

"You have more faith in the authorities than I do."

Freddie took a deep breath and tried not to look exasperated. "Okay, then talk to me about next steps."

"Next steps?"

"Yes, what are you going to do next?"

"Take the dog for a walk," Tree said.

"That's not much of a plan," Freddie said.

"But a very necessary step in this dog's life."

"I can't say I didn't try." She came over and kissed him on the mouth. "I've got to get to work. I hate to leave you here."

"I'll be fine," Tree said.

"Are we staying here tonight?"

Tree shrugged. "I'm not sure. I suppose we should."

"Okay, I'll get back as soon as I can. Maybe we can figure this out together."

"Bring some food, will you?"

"I'll see what I can do." She smiled and kissed him again. "Meanwhile, please stay out of trouble."

"I always try," Tree said.

"Try harder," Freddie replied.

———

By now it was apparent to Tree that, although he was surrounded by it, Clinton had no love for the water. He watched the dog bound along the sand, careful to skirt the incoming swell of the river, fearful of getting his paws wet. Clinton was definitely his kind of dog, Tree having much the same aversion to the water.

Clinton preferred searching out the infinite variety of landlocked scents. He turned abruptly and padded off the sand up onto a grassy patch offering new smells to be investigated. Why not just walk on beaches with Clinton for the rest of his days?

He could be content doing that. Beach walks with Clinton and lovemaking on boats with Freddie. As long as the boats were at a dock, and not bouncing around in the ocean. That would be a life. Carefree. The sort of thing he should be enjoying at his age. He was lost in the fantasy when his cellphone rang. He fished it out of his pocket.

"Mr. Callister?" a honey-dipped voice said.

"Yes?"

"Mr. Callister, this is T. Emmett Hawkins."

"Emmett Hawkins, the lawyer?" Hawkins was a prominent Fort Myers attorney who had represented one of Tree's clients.

"We've met before, Mr. Callister."

"Indeed we have, Mr. Hawkins. Not under the best of circumstances, I'm afraid."

"Well, in the business we are both in, people seldom meet under the best circumstances. If it were any different, we would be out of business."

"What can I do for you, Mr. Hawkins?"

"I'm returning your call, Mr. Callister."

"I wasn't calling you."

"I have a message here that says you called."

"Well, I didn't."

"The thing of it is, I've put aside an hour on my calendar. Why don't you drop around so we can talk? I have an hour free at eleven."

"Unfortunately, today, I don't have a car."

"I'll send my man to pick you up. Where are you located?"

"I'm at Gulf Harbor."

"My man will pick you up at 10:30 a.m. in front of the main clubhouse. I look forward to seeing you, Mr. Callister."

And before Tree could object further, T. Emmett Hawkins hung up.

28

Clinton returned to Tree, ears flopping, as if concerned his new friend might desert him. At least that was Tree's reading of what appeared to be Clinton's anxiousness. He bent down and rubbed the dog's chest. Clinton leaned against Tree's leg. "Don't worry, boy," Tree said. "No one's going to leave you."

Together, they walked back to the *Former Actor Too*, Tree thinking about the strange call from T. Emmett Hawkins. What could the lawyer possibly want with him?

He was about to find out.

Tree found a bowl in one of the cupboards that he filled with water. While the dog lapped it up, Tree tried the cramped little shower in the head. Not much luck there. The shower nozzle produced a dribble of water. The *Former Actor Too* was ill-prepared for overnight guests.

Tree stared at his unshaven visage in the tiny mirror above the sink. The light was all wrong. It made him look like an old man. Impossible. It had to be the lousy light, although as he shifted his gaze away from the mirror he had to concede that in his faded jeans, wrinkled gray T-shirt, and beat-up old deck shoes—clothes he had been wearing for twenty-four hours—he looked less the private investigator on his way to meet one of Fort Myers' most prestigious lawyers, and more like a beach bum asking for spare change.

An old beach bum? No. It was the bad lighting in the bathroom. He must talk to Rex and get him to fix that.

He hooked Clinton to his leash and led him off the boat along the dock to the drive that swung around the Gulf Harbor clubhouse. A black Range Rover was parked in front of the entrance. Leaning against its rear fender with his arms folded was a muscular Asian man, black hair close-cropped. The mustache and goatee lent a dangerous air to him. The beautifully cut Hugo Boss suit suggested the smart business professional.

As Tree approached, the Asian man straightened, unfolding his arms, eyeing the dog. "You are Tree Callister?" As though he didn't quite believe it.

"That's me," Tree said.

"You can't bring the dog," the driver said.

"I beg your pardon," Tree said.

"No dog. Not in the Range Rover."

"Why not?"

"I don't allow dogs in my Range Rover."

"This is your vehicle?"

The driver looked at him for a couple of beats before he said, "Dog gets hair all over the seat."

"Then I can't go with you," Tree said.

"Mr. Hawkins is waiting for you. I'm supposed to drive you to him."

"Not if I can't bring the dog."

The driver shifted around as though deciding whether or not to beat Tree to a pulp. He said, "Careful with that dog."

He opened the rear door to admit Tree. "Name's Lu," he said. "Spelled L-U. I don't like to be stereotyped."

"No," Tree said.

"You know, people thinking I'm this thing."

"This thing," Tree said.

"Because of the way I look. My look."

"Of course not," Tree said.

"I'm fighting against that," Lu said. "Even though, when it comes to taking care of things, I can take care of things. Know what I mean?"

"You take care of things," Tree said.

"I take care of things for Mr. Hawkins."

Clinton hopped nimbly into the rear seat. Tree slipped into the front while Lu eased himself behind the wheel and started the engine.

"But I'm only doing this temporarily," Lu said. "I'm actually a screenwriter."

"Is that so?" Tree said.

"I've written a script," Lu said. "An action thing. Hollywood wants action these days, you know."

"I didn't know," Tree said.

Lu swung the car around the drive and out to the Gulf Harbor entranceway. "I'm in the process of acquiring an agent, and after that it's a matter of time until one of the big studios grabs my script."

"Good luck with it." Tree couldn't think of anything else to say.

They rode in silence along McGregor Boulevard. "Just a matter of time," Lu said finally.

"But you haven't got an agent?"

"I'm *getting* an agent. No big deal. An agent. Then it goes to the studios."

"Well, like I said, good luck."

"It's a powerful script," Lu said. "Action. A dying American martial arts champion. Martial arts is huge in Asia. That's what's going to sell this baby. The Chinese are going to eat it up."

Tree turned to have a look at Clinton. He sat on his haunches, alert, mouth open, giving the distinct impression, Tree thought, that he was not buying a word out of Lu's mouth.

"I don't like dogs," Lu said.

"I'm sorry to hear that," Tree said.

"A dog bit me when I was a kid. Ever since then, me and dogs, hey, we just don't see eye to eye, know what I mean?"

"Clinton won't bite you," Tree reassured.

"Yeah, but he's getting hair all over the seat. I'm gonna have a time cleaning the car."

"Maybe your script will sell to a studio and you won't have to clean the car," Tree said.

"It's perfect for Mark."

"Mark?"

"Wahlberg. Mark Wahlberg." As though everyone should know. "He's an action guy. It's perfect for him."

"You know Mark?"

"The agent knows him."

"But you don't have an agent," Tree said.

Lu frowned and didn't say anything.

T. Emmett Hawkins occupied a suite of offices in an Art Deco building down the street from the Lee County Courthouse. Lu dropped Clinton and Tree off in front. Tree said to him, "Are you going to drive me back once I'm finished?"

"I've got to get the car cleaned," Lu said.

"What does that mean?"

Lu responded by driving away, leaving Tree and Clinton standing by the curb. Why should Lu care how he and Clinton were getting home? He was about to sell his script to Hollywood. All he needed was an agent. Then it was on to fame and fortune.

Tree went inside to a porcelain lobby with a receptionist who had full lips glistening with bright red lipstick. She said, "You can't bring that dog in here."

"Then I'm going to have to leave," Tree said.

"But Mr. Hawkins is waiting for you," she said unhappily. "I've had to juggle his calendar to fit you in."

"Then you're going to have to allow the dog to stay."

"Dogs aren't allowed in the building." The receptionist sounded unhappier now.

"It's up to you," Tree said.

She moved her red mouth around as though she had just tasted something unpleasant. Then she picked up the phone. "Hello, Mr. Hawkins. Yes, he's here. But he's got a dog with him." The receptionist fell silent and moved her mouth around some more. "I thought animals weren't allowed in the building. Yes, I see."

She hung up the phone and gave Tree a miserable look. "You can go back. Mr. Hawkins is waiting for you."

Hawkins occupied a large, book-lined room at the end of the hall. The window that interrupted the flow of the book-shelves framed the Lee County Courthouse, allowing Hawkins to contemplate the power of the law—or perhaps devise ways to defeat that power and keep his clients out of the jail behind the courthouse.

There was no desk, only a couple of dark leather sofas matching a pair of leather easy chairs, their backs bordered by brass studs. T. Emmett Hawkins, sleek and round, sporting his usual polka-dot bow tie, rose from one of the chairs, putting aside the papers he was studying. His shiny face broke into a welcoming smile. "There you are, Mr. Callister, so good to see you again."

He offered Tree a soft white hand.

"It's been a while, Emmett," Tree said.

"And who is this amiable-looking, long-eared fellow?" Hawkins bent forward for a closer inspection of Clinton. "Is it all right to pet him?"

Tree agreed that it was, and a soft white hand duly stroked Clinton's forehead. Clinton accepted the petting with his usual equanimity. "Good dog," Hawkins said. "Good boy."

"I don't think your driver likes dogs," Tree said.

"Yes, Lu," Hawkins said, concentrating on patting Clinton's head. "He's a character, is he not?"

Hawkins took his hand away and straightened to present Tree with one of his honey-dipped smiles. That voice, the soft smile. M. Emmett Hawkins was all Southern gentleman. Or at least that was the image he liked to present to the world.

"Won't you sit down, Mr. Callister? I'm so pleased my assistant was able to find a few moments for you."

Tree shook his head and said, "Emmett, I never called you."

Hawkins returned to one of the leather easy chairs. "Please do sit down," he said.

Tree seated himself across from Hawkins. Clinton made himself at home on the bamboo floor. "So what can I do for you, Emmett?"

"Perhaps it's what I can do for you, Mr. Callister."

"Is it?"

Hawkins formed his delicate white fingers into a tent and said, "I don't know if you're aware of my close relationship with Edith Goldman."

"I was aware that you were adversaries."

"That's the way it might have seemed, but in fact we were close friends. If I may say so, I was something of a mentor to Edith."

"I didn't know she needed a mentor," Tree said.

"Since her untimely death," Hawkins continued, "I have been entrusted with handling certain of Edith's affairs."

"When you speak of her untimely death, you mean her murder, don't you?"

Hawkins' face showed that he found the word "murder" unpleasant. "Yes, a tragedy to be sure," he said.

"Any idea who would have wanted to kill her?"

The tented fingers disappeared and reformed themselves into small fists, as if Hawkins might be willing to fight Tree over the question. But he answered courteously, choosing his words carefully. "If you are a defense attorney in this town, you can never be sure who or what you're going to run into," Hawkins said. "Edith had become involved with certain people, clients who, to say the least, were not of the best quality. In her eagerness to service those clients, she might have become involved in things she probably should not have become involved in."

"Vic Trinchera being one of those clients."

Hawkins paused long enough to look surprised. "Mr. Trinchera was a client of Edith's, that's true."

"And now Trinchera is dead."

Again Hawkins arranged to look surprised. "You're aware of this?"

"The Canadian gangster found dead in Miami. It was on the local news." Tree circumventing the truth once more. It appeared Hawkins knew nothing about Edith persuading him to meet with Trinchera.

Hawkins nodded and paused to contemplate the gravity of that statement before saying, "I don't know if you were aware of the high regard in which Edith held you, Mr. Callister."

"I liked Edith," Tree said truthfully. "She got me out of a couple of bad jams. I'm very sorry about what happened."

"I adored her. Another time, another place, well, who knows what might have happened between us. But the water is long since under that bridge, and has nothing to do with what brings us together today, does it?"

"I don't know, Emmett. What does bring us together?"

Hawkins appeared not to hear him. "But we must move on." He shifted in his chair, as if preparing to do exactly that. "As a result of Edith's death, I've taken on several of her clients. One of those clients is in need of the kinds of services Edith admired you for, Mr. Callister. The kinds of services I believe you could provide."

"I guess Edith forgot to tell you the part about me retiring."

Hawkins once again did not seem to hear Tree. "Knowing you wanted to see me today, I took the liberty to have my client drop around."

"Emmett, I don't know what you're up to, but I'm not taking on any more clients."

Hawkins rose to his feet. "This won't take long. I'd like the two of you to meet, and then you can decide for yourself."

Before Tree could issue further objections, Hawkins walked to a door at the side of the room and opened it. Almost immediately a man stepped in.

It was Vic Trinchera.

A dead man walking.

29

Clinton was on his feet, baring his teeth at the newcomer. "Keep that damn mutt away from me," the newcomer said in a warning voice.

"Mr. Callister, allow me to introduce you to Mr. Carmen Trinchera," T. Emmett Hawkins said.

Carmen Trinchera said, "My friends call me Sonny."

Tree took his offered hand. "You look a lot like your brother," he said.

"So everyone tells me," Sonny Trinchera said. "I don't see it myself."

Sonny Trinchera had the same long horse-face as his brother, the difference being he was dressed in a dark suit, unlike his track suit-clad brother, and unlike his brother, he wasn't wearing a Greek fisherman's cap to hide his baldness. Sonny wouldn't be playing bingo at a senior citizen's home, Tree decided. But in that suit he would be a great addition to your uncle's funeral.

"Mr. Trinchera has come from Montreal to make arrangements for his deceased brother," said Hawkins.

"My shot-to-death, dead brother," Sonny amended.

"I'm sorry to hear about your brother," Tree said.

"Kind of predictable, don't you think, given Vic's line of work? He was always no good, that guy. I knew some day he would buy a bullet. What I didn't figure is that it would happen in Florida. Just to make my life more complicated."

"I'm going to leave the two of you so that you can have a chat," Hawkins said.

"Yeah, why don't you do that?" Sonny Trinchera said.

"I'll come back in a few minutes."

Hawkins glided out of the office. Clinton remained on his feet, tail stiff, ears pricked, not moving.

"What's wrong with that dog?" Sonny Trinchera demanded.

"Clinton, settle down," Tree said. Clinton wasn't listening.

"I don't like dogs," Sonny said.

"Mr. Trinchera maybe you better tell me what you want," Tree said.

"Can you keep that mutt under control?"

"Is that what you want from me?"

Sonny gave Tree something that passed for a smile. "Funny guy," he said. "I suppose you think you're a funny guy, is that it?"

"I think we may be wasting each other's time."

"Let's go for a walk," Sonny Trinchera said.

"You're asking me to go for a walk?"

"I'm not asking," Sonny said.

By the time they got onto the street, Clinton had relaxed, or at least become too preoccupied with various sidewalk smells to worry about Sonny Trinchera.

They walked a couple of blocks until they reached the Tôt Funeral Home, a squat two-story whitewashed building jammed between a pizza joint and a jewelry store advertising gold and silver at prices that could not be beaten.

"This place is part of the funeral business I run in Canada and the United States," Sonny Trinchera said, opening the entrance door. "Follow me." He didn't sound as though he wanted to argue about it.

Inside, Sonny led Tree across a lobby to a long hall that ended at double doors. Sonny went through one of the doors, and Tree, leading Clinton, followed him into a high-ceilinged reception room, its hardwood floor covered with an intricately patterned Persian rug. The room was dark except for a shaft of light illuminating a golden coffin.

"I got him the best coffin money could buy," Sonny said. "The least I could do for my good-for-nothing brother. Gold on solid bronze. Fifty thousand dollars. How do you like that?"

"I'm sorry," was all Tree could think of to say.

"Don't feel sorry for this guy." Sonny rapped his knuckles against the coffin. "This guy brought nothing but shame to our family. We are a family of undertakers, the best—a reputation second to none in the Montreal area. But thanks to this guy, our name is forever tainted. People hear the name Trinchera, they don't hear respected funeral homes across the United States and Canada, they hear gangster."

Sonny Trinchera fell silent, glaring at his brother's expensive coffin. Clinton embarked upon a meticulous investigation around the table legs. Sniffing at the dead, Tree thought.

"I'm sorry you're going through this, Mr. Trinchera," he finally offered. His voice echoed in the room. "But I'm not quite sure how I can help you."

"I need someone local, an investigator who can help me track down the creep who whacked my brother. Hawkins says you're the guy for the job."

"I'm not the guy," Tree said. "This is the sort of thing the police are equipped to handle."

Sonny Trinchera made a derisive snorting sound. "Police," he said with a sneer. "You gotta be kidding me. The Miami police aren't gonna do anything. An old gangster from Montreal happens to get blown away in their town. Nothing to do with them. They're not going to spend any time on this." Sonny shook his head. "No, it's up to me to avenge my brother's death, and you're the guy who's gonna help me do it."

"Emmett should have told you that I'm retired," Tree said.

"For now, you are un-retired." Sonny Trinchera stated this with such certainty there seemed no point in arguing with him—as if arguing with Sonny might be a possibility.

"You know, Sonny, I don't know if anyone's ever told you this before, but the way you talk, someone might mistake *you* for the gangster."

"Nah, not me," he said. "I'm a mortician. That's all I am. Tôt Funeral Homes. U.S. and Canada branches. We take care of dead people."

"So supposing I find out who killed your brother, what do you propose to do about it?"

"Let's get out of here," Sonny said.

Clinton was on his feet, tail wagging, eager to leave. Tree put his hand on Sonny's arm. Sonny looked Tree up and down. "Did I mention this earlier? I don't like to be touched."

Tree took his arm away. "No, Sonny, you didn't say anything."

"In Montreal they know better. No one touches the Mortician."

"They call you the Mortician?"

"Not to my face, they don't."

"Okay, Sonny, it would be helpful if you could give me some sort of idea who you think might have killed your brother."

"I know who killed my brother."

"Who?"

"His mistress."

"Vic's mistress killed him?"

"What? You don't understand English? You got a problem with the language?"

"No, I understand what you're saying. You're saying it wasn't a mob hit?"

Sonny looked even more irritated. "Mob hit? What's all this crap about a mob hit? It wasn't no mob hit. It was that dame."

"What dame is that?"

"Melora Spark."

Tree hid his surprise with a question: "That's her name?"

"Yeah, that's her name."

"Who is she?"

"She's the dame who killed my brother."

"There must be more to her than that." Like maybe working as a Canadian Mountie, Tree thought.

"You don't need more. She's a tramp. A killer. End of story."

"It might be helpful to know where I can find this Melora Spark."

"He keeps her in an apartment down in Coral Gables. I'll give you the address."

"Okay. So what do you want me to do?"

Sonny looked impatient. "I want you to prove she killed my brother, what do you think I want you to do?"

"And just suppose, for the sake of argument, she didn't kill him."

"She did it. Don't you worry about that." Sonny glared at him. "All you got to do is worry about pleasing me."

He reached inside his suit jacket and pulled out a wad of money held together by a rubber band.

"There's five thousand dollars," Sonny said. "That should get you started. There's more when you get results."

"I can't take this," Tree said.

"Why not?"

"Because I'm not at all sure I can get you the results you're after."

"That's not what I want to hear." Sonny's voice was hard. He shoved the money into Tree's hands "I don't like hearing things I don't want to hear."

Tree gave Sonny back the money. "Then let's make sure I'm in a position to tell you something you want to hear."

"Fair enough," Sonny said. "You please the Mortician, everything's hunky-dory. You don't please the Mortician . . ."

"Everything's not hunky-dory?"

"Say, you may not be as dumb as you look." Sonny Trinchera cracked a smile.

The wad of bills disappeared back inside his jacket.

30

Freddie returned to the *Former Actor Too* that night carrying a couple of grocery bags. Tree came to meet her on the dock and took the bags on board. Clinton gave himself a good shake before happily jumping up on Freddie. She rubbed his ears and said, "What we're doing for you, puppy dog, hiding out on a boat, eating out of cans. I hope you appreciate it."

Tree found a cold bottle of chardonnay in one of the bags, used a corkscrew to pull the cork, and poured her a glass. They sat together on the deck, Clinton lying beside Freddie. Tree filled her in on the day's confusing series of events involving the unexpected appearance of Vic Trinchera's brother, Sonny.

"Let me get this straight," Freddie said. "Neither Emmett Hawkins nor Sonny Trinchera appear to know anything about Clinton?"

"What's more, they showed no interest," Tree added. "In fact when Clinton saw Sonny, he growled."

"Unusual for Clinton," Freddie said.

At the mention of his name, Clinton raised his head and quizzically regarded his two companions.

"Sonny said he doesn't like dogs."

"But Sonny does think that Melora Spark is Vic's girlfriend, and she killed his brother."

"Melora, supposedly a member of the Royal Canadian Mounted Police, now has been recast as Vic's killer," Tree said.

"The Case of the Murderous Mistress," Freddie said.

"According to Sonny."

"But how does he know?"

"He just knows, that's all there is to it. No arguing the point. What's more, he has hired me to prove it."

"Tree, you can't do this."

"Right now, I'm not sure I've got a whole lot of choice."

"Yes, you do. Go to the police."

"First of all, I need to know why everyone is after this guy." He pointed to Clinton. "Until someone tells me that, I'm not willing to give him up."

"I'm beginning to wonder if you're willing to give him up, period."

"Maybe we won't have to."

"Tree."

"I'm just saying."

"He's not our dog."

Tree didn't say anything. He busied himself petting Clinton. The dog stretched in luxurious contentment. How was he ever going to give this guy up? Tree wondered.

He would worry about that later.

———————

Tree prepared a salad while Freddie seared a couple of tuna steaks in the *Former Actor Too*'s galley. They ate out on the deck, alternately watching the sun set and Clinton enthusiastically chowing down the kibble Freddie had brought to the boat.

When they finished, they took Clinton for a long walk around Gulf Harbor. As usual, he attracted a lot of attention, everyone stopping to pet him, everyone wanting to know his name and asking what kind of dog he was. Clinton took it all in stride; stardom didn't bother him in the least.

Returning to the boat, Freddie treated herself to a second glass of chardonnay while Tree cleaned up the dishes as best he could, given the limitations of the narrow kitchen featuring a tap that made a thumping sound but refused to yield anything more than a feeble stream of lukewarm water.

They settled once again into *Former Actor Too*'s comfortable bed with Clinton stretched out between them. Shards of moonlight filtered through the cabin. The waters of the Caloosahatchee River were gentle against the bow of the boat, relaxing Tree as he drifted off, believing against his natural instincts that all was not so bad with the world.

Except for that noise.

Clinton lifted his head, his ears perking up.

Something moving. On the deck above them. Clinton growled and jumped off the bed. Tree threw back the covers. Freddie sat up sleepily. "What is it?"

"I'm just going to see," Tree whispered, slipping out of bed. "Stay where you are."

"Tree, don't do anything crazy."

Tree stood very still, listening.

The sound of feet softly on the rear deck was quickly followed by a clatter as whoever was up there crashed into a deck chair.

That started Clinton barking.

Tree grabbed the dog by the collar, holding him. With his free hand he threw open the cabin door and called out, "Whoever's up there—I've got a gun!"

A voice called back: "No way. You don't have a gun."

Tree let go of Clinton who went barking and scrambling up the stairs. By the time Tree reached the deck, Clinton was wagging his tail, presenting himself to Rex Baxter's hand.

Rex turned toward Tree and grinned crookedly. "See? I knew you didn't have a gun. Anywhere else in South Florida, there would have been a gun. But my old friend, W. Tremain Callister, he would not have a gun."

Rex stumbled a bit before he slumped down on one of the deck seats. He gave Tree another crazy grin. "I thought maybe you'd like to have a drink with your pal. Like the old days. You and me, we had lots of drinks back then. Too many. We became friends over drinks. Do you remember?"

"I was going to say something about hoping you didn't drive here," Tree said. "But I guess I would be wasting my breath."

"How about that drink?" Rex said.

Tree called down to Freddie. "It's okay, honey. It's Rex."

"Rex?" Her voice came up from below. "What's Rex doing here at this time of night?"

"Tell her I'm looking for a drink."

"You've come to the wrong place," Tree said to him.

Rex shook his head lazily. "No, I'm at the absolute *right* place. I left a bottle of vodka under the sink."

"I don't think you need any more to drink," Tree said.

"That's where you are wrong. I need a whole lot more. That's why I'm here. To drink a whole lot more."

Freddie emerged from the cabin dressed in shorts and a T-shirt. "Rex, are you crazy?" she said.

"Just a little drunk," Rex said. "Sorry about this, Freddie. I needed to talk to old friends. Someone who has known me since the earth cooled. Your husband happens to fit the profile."

"Are you all right?"

"I'm in dramatic mode tonight. Kelly and I had a fight."

"What did you fight about?" Freddie asked.

"Your husband."

Freddie looked at him. "Why would you fight over Tree?"

"Because maybe, just maybe, I'm jealous of him."

Freddie ruffled Rex's hair. "No need to be jealous. He belongs to me."

"Now and forever," Tree said.

She bent forward to kiss Rex on the cheek. "Love you though I do, my dear, I've got to get up first thing in the morning. I'm leaving you in good sober hands—and paws."

"I'm not so sure Clinton's sober," Rex said.

"Good night, you two," Freddie said. She gave Tree a quick kiss and said, "Don't do or say anything to make Rex jealous. Understand?"

"Roger that," Tree said.

Freddie disappeared into the cabin.

"You should stay here the night," Tree said.

"I've got to get home," Rex said. "Home to the lovely, elusive Kelly."

"Come on, be honest. You didn't really get into a fight over me."

"You kissed her, didn't you?"

"I didn't kiss her," Tree said.

"She kissed you."

"It was a kiss, but it wasn't a kiss," Tree said.

"It looked like a kiss to me," Rex said.

"It wasn't anything," Tree insisted.

"Tell me this," Rex said. "Did you love her?"

"Love who?"

"You know who I'm talking about. Did you love Kelly?"

"That's probably not a question you should ask a guy who's been married four times."

"But I'm asking you, Tree."

He thought about it and then said, "I don't think it was a question of whether I loved her. I think the problem was she stopped loving me."

"She says she doesn't think you ever loved her."

"What can I say, Rex. That would not be my read of the situation. Not that it makes any difference at this point."

They fell silent. Various night sounds floated across the stern of the *Former Actor Too*. In the distance, Tree heard the thin sound of a passing car on McGregor Boulevard. Rex rubbed his hand across his face, a gesture he had not seen his old friend perform since their Chicago days when there was ratings pressure at WBBM-TV. Or a former wife was complaining about a late alimony payment. Or one of his kids was in trouble.

"You see, the thing of it is, I am crazy about this woman— this woman who is your ex-wife. This woman I introduced you to, for God's sake."

"Only Kelly could get you drunk and keep you up this late at night."

"What I can't tell, the unsolved mystery, I can't tell how this woman, this ex-wife of yours, feels about me." He rubbed his face again and then looked blearily at Tree. "How do you know that, Tree? How can you tell—how did you know when Freddie was crazy about you?"

"Easy enough. She told me."

That reduced Rex to another bout of silence and more face massaging. "There you go," Rex said finally. "That's it, isn't it?"

"The only thing I would say, and it's kind of late at night and you're sort of out of it, Rex, but for you and Kelly it's still early days. Relax and enjoy what the two of you have, and sort of let it develop from there."

"I don't think she likes me," he said.

"That's crazy," Tree said. "How can you say she doesn't like you?"

"Okay, maybe she *likes* me, but that's as far as it goes. I irritate her, I think. At least she gives me that impression."

"Everybody irritates Kelly from time to time," Tree said. "She's an impatient woman, and she's floundering right now. For years her identity was built around being a Chicago TV personality. She loved it, loved all the attention."

"I know she did," Rex said. "Who didn't?"

"Now she's lost that, and she's suffering."

"She could be happy with me," Rex said. "I could make her happy."

"I think you would make her a lot happier if you didn't stay out late and get drunk. She must be concerned and wondering where you are."

"I don't think she gives a damn," Rex said.

"Of course she does."

He shook his head in wonderment. "First time I've had a fight with a woman in I don't know how many years. I'd forgotten how sick it can make you feel."

"I'm going to drive you home, Rex. This will all look different in the morning."

"What? You can't stay up and talk to an old buddy about his woman troubles?"

"It's late, and I've got a full day tomorrow."

"Full day? Hey, you're retired, remember?"

"Yeah, right," Tree said, getting to his feet. "Sometimes I forget."

"Tree Callister. The ex-Sanibel Sunset detective. So much for reinvention. Didn't work out so well, did it?"

Tree said, "Give me your car keys, Rex."

"I'm okay to drive," Rex said. "I don't need some retired guy driving me around."

"Come on. Don't argue. Hand over the keys."

Rex sighed and groped in his pocket. "It's not keys anymore," he said. "It's a key. And it's not even a key."

He tossed the key to Tree. He tried his best to catch it, but he fumbled the catch. Rex chortled. "You never were any good at sports. You were never much good at anything—except you were a pretty damned good reporter." Rex paused and thought about it. "There is one other thing you're good at."

"Being a detective?" Tree said.

"No, you're not much of a detective, either. I'll tell you what you're good at, Tree. You're very good at being my friend."

"Then I don't need much more than that," Tree said.

He helped Rex to his feet.

31

The driver's side door of Rex's prized Dodge Challenger Hellcat had been left open in the lot adjacent to the Gulf Harbor clubhouse. Tree got Rex into the passenger seat and then went around and slipped behind the wheel. Rex was snoring by the time he started the engine. It was like awakening a monster in its cave. The sound of that motor made Tree nervous. He gripped the T shifter and shoved it into reverse. The Hellcat jerked back and brought Rex awake. He sat up groggily. "What are you doing?" he said in a slurry voice.

"I'm driving you home."

"You don't have to do that," he said. "I'm okay."

"I know, but humor me, will you?"

"Okay. Ordinarily, I wouldn't let you behind the wheel of this Hellcat. But it's in valet mode right now, so I guess it's okay."

"Valet mode?"

"It means no one but me can drive it full out."

"Good. I don't want to drive this thing full out," Tree said.

Rex reached forward and fumbled with the glove compartment. The lid dropped down with a loud clunk. He pulled the gun out and held it up so that the otherworldly glow from the dashboard touchscreen gleamed off its surface.

"What's that?" Tree said.

"You're fairly new to South Florida, so you wouldn't know. This is what the locals call an equalizer. Folks from out of state refer to it as a gun. The Glock 17, the weapon of choice for police officers all over America."

"Except you're not a police officer. What are you doing with it?"

"What do you think I'm doing? I'm protecting myself—and my Hellcat."

"Why don't you put the gun back where you found it?"

"Do I make you nervous?"

"You don't. The gun does."

"You should get yourself one of these babies."

"Please, Rex. Do me a favor. Put it away."

Rex made a grumbling sound, but he replaced the Glock in the glove compartment. Tree breathed a sigh of relief. Rex's head fell back against the headrest and a couple of moments later he resumed his loud snoring.

There was little traffic at that time of the morning as Tree guided the Dodge Challenger across the causeway onto Sanibel Island. Rex's place was dark as Tree pulled into the drive. He turned off the engine, and nudged his sleeping friend. He snapped awake. "Yeah? What is it?"

"We're home."

"How did we get here?"

"I drove you."

"Are you out of your mind? The Hellcat's not in valet mode."

"I thought you said it was."

"Nobody but me can drive this car. For everyone else, it's valet mode."

Tree got out and went around to the passenger side and helped Rex out. He practically had to drag his friend up to the front door. "Now what are you doing?" Rex demanded.

"Making sure you get home safely."

"That used to be my job with you," Rex said.

"Many times, old friend. Many times."

The front door opened and a tousled-looking Kelly stood there in a white bathrobe. She cocked an eyebrow and said, "Here is something I never thought I'd see. My ex-husband, sober, bringing my drunk boyfriend home late at night."

"I ended up drunk," Rex said. "Must have been something I ate."

Kelly sighed. "What is it about me that drives men to drink—don't answer that, Tree. Just bring him inside, please."

"I'm okay," Rex protested. "A little wobbly, that's all. It's this cold. I haven't been able to shake it."

Tree helped his friend through the house, past the gigantic poster of *I Died A Thousand Times*, Rex's only concession to his long-ago life as a Hollywood B-movie actor. One half of the king-size bed had been slept in. Kelly squeezed past and pulled back the covers to allow Tree to perch Rex on the mattress. Rex sat there for a couple of moments, picking absently at the buttons of his shirt. Then he gave up and sank back and started to snore.

Kelly stared down at the sleeping Rex. To Tree's surprise, her features were soft with concern. "This business of relationships is hard on Rex," she said. "I think he finds it a whole lot easier to play the hail-fellow-well-met president of the Chamber of Commerce."

She looked up from Rex and turned her gaze on Tree, as if expecting him to say something.

"He'll sleep it off" was all Tree could think of to say.

"Yes," she said. "He will do that. Men always do. They always sleep it off."

"I'd better get back," Tree said.

She followed him out of the bedroom. At the front door she put her hand on his arm and said, "Thanks for bringing him home."

"Tell him I stole his car," Tree said. "He can pick it up tomorrow."

"He's overreacting to a silly little fight," she said.

"He's crazy about you," Tree said. "You know that, don't you?"

"Yes, of course."

"That makes him vulnerable, and Rex isn't used to that, not around these parts. Here he's pampered."

"What about you, Tree? Are you pampered, too?"

Tree smiled. "I'm not in Rex's league. I'm still out there in the world fighting the dragons."

"That's what makes you an interesting story."

"I doubt it," Tree said.

"So you're not hiding out on Rex's boat?"

"Let's put it this way. Until we get the house straightened around, we're staying on the boat."

"Have it your way," Kelly said. "But I know there's a story, and I'm going to get it out of you."

"In the meantime, take care of our boy, will you?"

"I'll do my best," Kelly said. "But I'm not sure what he needs."

"A little love would probably do the trick," Tree said.

Kelly gave a tired smile and squeezed his arm. "Thanks again, Tree."

32

He might have said a lot of things to Kelly, he thought as he drove back along deserted Periwinkle Way.

He could have asked her, for example, what she was doing with her life, and question whether a relationship with Rex Baxter was really in the best interest of either party. Kelly, he suspected, was never going to commit herself fully, not in the way lonely Rex wanted a commitment. But then what did he know about Kelly so many years after their marriage? And what business was it of his, anyway? They were adults. They could take care of themselves. Well, mostly they could take care of themselves. Every once in a while, Rex might need help.

Like right now.

The guard on duty at Gulf Harbor recognized Tree, glanced appreciatively at the Hellcat, before lifting the gate to allow him inside. He drove to the parking lot adjacent to the clubhouse and got out of the vehicle, stretching his cramped legs. Exhaustion washed over him. He took a deep breath. The night air smelled clean. The stars sparkled against a clear black sky, distracting the onlooker from the view of three figures darting out of the shadows and onto the dock.

Tree watched the three forms in the darkness, allowing the reality of them to sink in. He wheeled back to the Hellcat for Rex's Glock. Maybe it wasn't such a bad idea, after all.

He came onto the dock. The three forms huddled close by the *Former Actor Too*. They were in black and in the uncertain light, their faces appeared to be covered by Mexican wrestling masks decorated with skulls. They turned in surprise as Tree approached. His heart beat so fast and loud, he was sure the intruders would hear and know he wasn't much of a threat.

"What can I do for you?" he called to them.

The men didn't say anything for a time, as though deciding what Tree could do for them. Then one called out in a raspy voice: "Is this boat for sale?"

Tree realized with a start this had to be Raspy-voice Guy.

"You want to buy a boat at this time of morning?"

"Best time to look," Raspy-voice Guy said. "No traffic."

"If I were you, I wouldn't go looking for a boat wearing masks," Tree observed. He further noted Pockmarked Guy was not wearing a straw hat, so it was difficult to identify him or Balding Guy for that matter. But he had no doubt as to their identities. "What are those? Mexican wrestling masks?"

"We're Mexican wrestlers," Raspy-voice guy said.

"I thought so," Tree said.

"All right, then, why don't you just give us the dog and we'll leave you alone."

"I don't know what dog you're talking about," Tree said.

From inside the boat, Clinton began to bark.

"That dog," said Raspy-voice Guy.

"That's a cat," Tree said.

"We will take the cat," Raspy-voice Guy said.

Tree raised his hand so that the intruders could see the moonlit Glock. "No," he said. "You won't."

"No need for that," said Raspy-voice Guy in a reasonable voice.

"That's what I keep telling myself," Tree said.

"We don't want trouble. No one gets hurt—if we take the dog."

"Tell me something," Tree said. "What's the big deal about the dog? Why do you want him so badly?"

"You tell me," Raspy-voice Guy replied. "You're the one willing to shoot people in order to hang onto him."

Freddie appeared on the aft deck holding tight to a barking, snarling Clinton.

"Tree?" Freddie called. "Are you all right?"

"Yes, come off the boat, Freddie."

"Why are these guys standing there?"

"Because if they do anything, I'm going to shoot them."

"You're kidding," Freddie said. "What are you doing with a gun?"

"Just come off the boat, Freddie. Step off the back and be careful."

Freddie did as she was instructed. The three men didn't move—the power of the gun. Freddie joined Tree on the dock. Clinton, held taut on his leash, lunged and barked.

"I can't believe you have a gun," Freddie said. "Where did you get a gun?"

Tree said, "Freddie, I want you to take the key I'm going to hand you, and then I want you to go up to the parking lot, start the car, and bring it as close to the dock as you can. As soon as you've done that, I want you to sound the horn. Okay?"

Freddie pulled Clinton away and hurried off the dock into the darkness. Tree started backing away from the trio.

"This is the part where I say, Stay where you are," Tree said.

"I don't think you're going to shoot anyone," Raspy-voice Guy said.

"I've been thinking about it," Tree said. "And you know what? I honestly don't know for sure. But it's probably the wrong time to test me."

Raspy-voice Guy said, "You're going to be in a world of trouble, friend."

"I'm not your friend," Tree said.

"Not after tonight, you're not," Raspy-voice Guy said.

Tree continued to back slowly away along the dock, keeping his gun arm outstretched. The sound of a car horn broke the silence. Tree reached the end of the dock, turned and ran up past the clubhouse to where Freddie waited with the Hellcat's motor running, headlights shining through the night. Freddie had already opened the passenger door so he could hop in.

"Drive," he said, slamming the door.

Freddie stepped on the gas. She screamed in alarm as the Hellcat practically went into orbit, fishtailing violently around. Freddie, fighting with the wheel, lifted her foot off the gas pedal, allowing the Hellcat to right itself. She reapplied gas and the car shot forward with a screech of burning rubber. "Good grief," she said as they roared out the driveway. "What's under the hood?"

"Seven hundred bucking, kicking horses," Tree said. "A man's car."

"It's at times like this that I'm glad I'm a woman," Freddie said.

From the backseat, Clinton uttered a whimper. Tree reached back to pet him. "It's all right, sweetheart," he said softly. "It's going to be all right."

"Tree," Freddie said, "it's the middle of the night, you've got a gun in your hand, and we're running away from guys wearing funny skeleton masks. How can anything be all right?"

Tree had no answer.

33

The desk clerk at the Comfort Inn off I-75 didn't bat an eyelash when Freddie and Tree told him they had no luggage. In the not-too-distant past, Tree with no luggage in the company of a beautiful woman trying to check into a hotel, his heart would have been in his mouth. In this new and wondrous century, he simply handed the desk clerk a credit card. A credit card even made a dog at three o'clock in the morning welcome.

"Those were Johnny Bravo's people, weren't they?" Freddie said when they were in the room.

"Our old pals," Tree said.

Freddie said, "I don't know what they were trying to prove with those masks."

"They were trying to fool us," Tree said.

"Well, they didn't succeed."

Clinton had already commandeered the center of the huge bed, resting on his haunches, large eyes shifting back and forth between Freddie and Tree, wondering why they were not coming to bed at this late hour. The dog, Tree was beginning to think, was a whole lot smarter than they were.

"And what about that gun? How did you get your hands on a gun?"

"It belongs to Rex."

"Where is it now?"

"I left it in the glove compartment," Tree said.

"Good, because I don't like you with a gun. Guns make me very nervous."

"They make me nervous, too. But I have to admit we would have been in a lot of trouble tonight without it."

"What's Rex doing with a gun? What's he need it for?"

"He's trying to assimilate into South Florida life. He bought a boat. Maybe he thought he needed a gun, too."

"I hate this being on the run," Freddie said. "There's too much going on at work for me to become a desperado."

"Desperado," Tree said. "I like that word. A couple of desperadoes—like Bonnie and Clyde."

"We are too old to be Bonnie and Clyde," Freddie said, gently shifting Clinton around so she could pull down the bed covers. "And besides, Bonnie and Clyde didn't have a dog."

"They'd have been much better off if they did," Tree said.

Freddie stretched out beside Clinton who responded by rolling onto his back so that all four paws dangled in the air. Freddie reached over and stroked his belly.

"I shouldn't be falling for you, Clinton," she said to him. "This is so crazy. We are hiding out because of a dog. If we told anyone that our lives have been totally upended for a hound, they would think we are nuts—and they would be right. We are nuts. That's the only possible explanation."

"There's another explanation," Tree said.

Freddie said, "What's the other explanation?"

"You're married to me."

"That still qualifies as nuts."

"I'm the cause of all this. I keep getting you into these messes."

"Okay, but don't think that's an excuse. I'm still not going to divorce you."

"That's the good news," Tree said.

"Even though it turns out you're armed and dangerous."

"Well, I'm armed," Tree said.

"I don't like you armed," she said. Her voice had dropped to a murmur. "I like the retired Tree Callister, unarmed citizen of the world."

He finished undressing and crawled in on the other side of Clinton. "For now, let's get some sleep. I'm having trouble keeping my eyes open."

When Freddie didn't respond, he raised himself up on his elbow and saw that already she had fallen asleep, her hand still on Clinton.

Tree lay down. Beside him, Clinton shifted contentedly, his paws poking at Tree's chest. Tree drifted off, stroking Clinton's belly.

———————

At ten o'clock the next morning, Freddie shot upright, announcing her panic at the lateness of the hour. During what was left of the night, Clinton had stretched out his long spindly legs, commandeering most of the available space, pushing Tree and Freddie to the outer extremities of the bed.

Freddie trailed a series of complaints as she headed for the bathroom. The complaints included the fact that she was in a Comfort Inn with a dog and a husband and no toothbrush, no makeup, no change of clothes. She called down to the desk and had someone send up toothpaste and a toothbrush.

The toothbrush arrived as Freddie was in the shower and at the moment when Tree's cellphone sounded. He was immediately sorry he answered it.

"Have you found my brother's killer yet?" Sonny Trinchera at full snarl.

"How did you get this number?"

"When I want things, I get things. Have you found his killer or not?"

"Sonny, come on, I haven't even had my coffee," Tree said.

"I'm looking for results," Sonny said. "I'm not a patient guy."

"I didn't get much sleep last night, thanks to a visit from three bruisers in Mexican wrestling masks."

Sonny hesitated before he said, "What's a Mexican wrestling mask?"

"Masks worn by Mexican wrestlers."

"Why would they wear masks?"

"Do you know someone named Johnny Bravo?"

"Never heard of him."

"That's funny. He's supposed to be a well-known Montreal gangster."

"I'm a mortician. I don't know anything about gangsters."

"So you keep telling me," Tree said.

"What did these clowns want, anyway?"

Tree decided this was not the time to tell Sonny about a dog named Clinton who seemed to be on everyone's must-have list except Sonny's. Instead, he said, "Maybe they wanted to know what I'm doing connected to you."

"How would they know we're connected?"

"I don't know, but I no sooner am mixed up with you than these characters show up."

"You didn't tell them anything, did you?" Sonny sounded deeply suspicious.

"I told them to go to hell," Tree said, feeling very much the tough guy first thing in the morning.

Sonny now sounded skeptical. "Three guys wearing masks show up in the middle of the night, and you tell them to go to hell? Hey, don't kid a kidder."

"That's what I told them."

"Then why aren't you dead or in the hospital?"

"I had a gun."

That reduced Sonny to unaccustomed silence. When he spoke again there was a little more respect in his voice. "Maybe I underestimated you, Callister."

"If you had that low an estimation of me, Sonny, why did you hire me in the first place?"

"Phone me as soon as you get results," Sonny said. And then he was gone.

By now, Clinton was sitting up, his head slightly cocked, watching as Freddie appeared from the bathroom, naked and dripping wet from the shower. "Who was that?"

"My new best friend, Sonny Trinchera."

"What did he want?"

"He wanted to know why I haven't found his brother's killer."

"What did you tell him?"

"I asked him what he knew about three characters wearing Mexican wrestling masks late at night."

"What did he say?"

"He wanted to know what a Mexican wrestling mask was."

"I've got to get out of here," Freddie said, grabbing the toothbrush and toothpaste off the dresser where Tree had placed them. "Can you be ready to leave in ten minutes?"

———————

After dropping Freddie off at Dayton's, Tree and Clinton drove to the Chamber of Commerce Visitors Center. Clinton followed him in the back door and up the stairs Tree had climbed so many times. His office was as he had left it. The pencil sharpener and the Scotch tape—property of the Chamber—had not been moved. Awaiting his return?

No, Tree thought. Don't even think about it.

Clinton shuffled around the office while Tree sat behind the desk. It felt unexpectedly good to be sitting there. Why, he could even pretend to be a detective. He quickly dismissed those thoughts. He was retired. On the run, but retired.

He picked up the telephone and called Jim Devereaux in Montreal.

Devereaux said, "What's going on down there? I hear they knocked off André Manteau."

"That's what I understand," Tree said.

"I got reports that the Miami cops found him in a beaten-up Volkswagen registered to a certain Sanibel Sunset detective."

"One of these days, I'll tell you the whole story."

"I'm looking forward to that," Devereaux said. "There appears to be a whole lot more to you than I would have suspected from a guy crazy enough to be a detective on Sanibel Island."

"What can you tell me about a man named Sonny Trinchera?"

"Carmen Trinchera, known to everyone as Sonny," Devereaux said. "Don't tell me he's down there."

"He's in town to bury his brother."

"The Mortician at work," Devereaux said. "Although I'm sure he isn't shedding many tears."

"He doesn't appear to be," Tree said. "Is he a gangster, too?"

"Sonny always claims he isn't," Devereaux said. "He operates the funeral homes that he and his brother own throughout the province of Quebec, and also in New York State and Florida."

"Okay, he says he isn't a gangster, Jim. But what do you say?"

Devereaux chuckled. "I always get a kick out of Sonny's protestations that he is, and I'm quoting here, 'clean as the driven snow.' But nobody I talk to in organized-crime circles believes it. I'd say at the very least, he moves easily through his brother's world. Incidentally, there has always been quite a rivalry between them. If you believe the rumors, Sonny wouldn't mind taking over the Montreal mob and running it himself. He certainly thinks he could do a better job than either his brother or Johnny Bravo. Why are you so interested in Sonny?"

"He hired me the other day."

"To do what?"

"Find his brother's killer."

"I don't believe it," Devereaux said.

"That's what he wants me to do—and he wants results ASAP."

"That sounds like Sonny all right."

Tree thought for a minute. "Let me throw another name at you," Tree said.

"Shoot," said Devereaux.

"Shay Ostler. Does that name mean anything to you?"

"Not a thing," Devereaux said.

"She was working for André Manteau before he died. They may have been linked romantically as well. But since his death, no one's even mentioned her."

"The name doesn't ring any bells, but just for fun, let me dig around, see what I can find."

"I appreciate this, Jim."

"Be careful, Tree. You are down there messing with some pretty dangerous people."

———————

Rex entered, carrying a Styrofoam tray containing two Starbucks Grande Lattes. He wore dark glasses this morning. He handed one of the cups to Tree and sat down in the chair in front of the desk. Clinton came over, looking to be petted. Rex obliged.

"You're missed around here," Rex said. "It's not every Chamber of Commerce that has its own private detective on the premises."

"How do you feel?"

"Like a bag of dirt," Rex said.

Tree took the Glock out of his pocket and placed it on the desk in front of Rex. "I brought your gun back."

"Thanks," Rex said.

Tree said, "How did you know I'd be here this morning?"

"I figured you'd come in to give me hell."

"Not me," Tree said.

"I'm a stupid old fart," Rex said, giving Clinton another pat.

"On occasion, I'd say that's true," Tree said.

"By the way, I went around to the boat this morning. Looks like someone trashed it pretty good. Either that, or you and Freddie had one hell of a party after you drove me home."

"I'm sorry, Rex. We had some unexpected visitors last night. I thought I'd convinced them to leave."

"How did you do that?"

"I showed them your gun."

Rex sipped his coffee and petted Clinton some more. "Correct me if I'm wrong, but I keep thinking you're retired."

"I keep thinking the same thing," Tree said. "However, I might be mistaken. That's why I need your help today."

"How can I say no," said Rex.

"I'm going to steal your Hellcat, and I need you to look after Clinton until I get back."

"My brand-new sixty-thousand-dollar, fire-engine red, Dodge Charger Hellcat?"

"That's the one," Tree said.

"This is a question I've asked you before," Rex said.

"Yes," Tree said.

"Are you sure you know what you're doing?"

"How have I answered that question in the past?"

"Usually in the negative."

"Good," Tree said. "I see no reason to change that answer. Make sure you take good care of Clinton, will you?"

"Better take this with you." Rex pushed the Glock across the desk toward Tree.

"I'm tough without a gun," Tree said.

"That's Humphrey Bogart," Rex said. "I've got some bad news for you."

"What's that?"

"You're no Bogart."

Tree stared at the gun.

34

The Miracle Mile in Coral Gables was a mile long, but not much of a miracle. Lackluster storefront windows were mostly devoted to white wedding gowns for tradition-minded brides-to-be with piles of money to spend on the Big Day. No brides that Tree could see at this time of the morning, though, just a few pedestrians in what Freddie would describe as business casual exiting and entering a nearby Starbucks.

Tree turned the Hellcat off the Miracle Mile onto Ponce de León and then made another left onto Navarre Avenue. The address Sonny Trinchera had given him was a three-story white-washed apartment building on the corner. The strip fronting the façade was choked with bushes and small palms facing a metered parking lot across the street. Tree pulled into the lot and positioned the car so that he had an unobstructed view of the street and the apartment building. He turned off the engine, snapped open the Diet Coke he had brought with him, and settled in.

For the first hour or so no one came in or out of the building. Tree, as he usually did during these watches, contemplated the waste of his life. After he had thoroughly beaten himself up, he grew drowsy and fought to keep his eyes open.

Into the second hour, he got out and walked along the block. It was a glorious morning in South Florida, a breeze cooling the warming effects of a bright sun in a cloudless sky. At the end of the street, he paused, listening to the insects and distant traffic sounds. For all he knew, he was the only person left in South Florida.

He turned to start back and that's when he saw the black and yellow Ducati Streetfighter motorcycle pull up in front of the apartment building. The rider removed a black Daft Punk helmet. He watched as Shay Ostler shook her hair loose, the way she had done it the first time Tree met her at Crimson's studio. Then, carrying the helmet, she got off the motorcycle and went inside.

Tree ran back to the Hellcat. He didn't have to wait long before Shay Ostler emerged from the building. Melora Spark was with her.

For one worrying moment, Tree thought they would walk straight across to where he was parked. Instead, they stopped at Shay's Streetfighter. She put on her helmet while Melora eased herself onto the passenger seat. A moment later the bike roared to life, and Shay, with Melora's arms wrapped around her, shot off down the block.

Tree started the Hellcat, swung it around, and drove after them.

They didn't go very far, straight down Southwest Forty-second Avenue and then right on Anastasia to the Biltmore Hotel. The Streetfighter swung into the parking lot beside the hotel. Tree watched Shay and Melora get off the bike and walk toward a side entrance.

Tree parked in the street adjacent to the parking lot. He opened the glove compartment containing the Glock, thought about it, then closed the glove compartment again and got out of the car.

The Biltmore lobby with its vaulted ceilings and artfully potted palms was as cool and empty as it was the last time he visited. Wherever the denizens of Coral Gables escaped, it was not to the lobby of the Biltmore.

There was no sign of Shay and Melora in any of the cabanas adjacent to the pool, so he went up some steps to the terrace. They were seated at the other end with Johnny Bravo. Tree debated what to do, then decided he had come this far, and, taking a deep breath, he walked to their table.

To his credit, Johnny managed not to look surprised when he saw Tree approach. Melora satisfied herself with a frown,

Tree being one more irritant in a day full of them. Shay gave him a cool, appraising look, as if her beauty would not permit her to be surprised by anything as controllable as a man.

"There you are, Tree Callister, Monsieur Detective," Johnny Bravo called, as though a long lost friend had arrived for lunch. "Come. Join us. You're just in time. We're about to order."

Tree sat on the empty wrought iron chair between Melora and Shay. Melora held a large menu, but ignored it and kept her eyes on Tree. "What are you doing here?"

"It looks like I'm having lunch with you."

Johnny Bravo raised his hand and called to a distant waiter. "Could we have another menu, please?"

The waiter, a young man with thinning blond hair, hurried over and handed Tree a menu. "Can I get you something to drink, sir?" he said.

Tree asked for a glass of water, and the waiter scurried away.

"What? No wine?" Johnny Bravo said. "I guess I am not in Montreal, am I?"

"Tree, you shouldn't be here," Melora said.

"I'm not so sure about that, Sergeant," Tree said equably. "This could be an opportunity for the four of us to be a little more honest with each other than we have up until now. I know that Johnny is a gangster. That's clear enough."

"I'm a Montreal businessman," Johnny protested. "I have nothing to do with gangsters."

"But I'm not so sure about you, Melora. Are you really a member of the Royal Canadian Mounted Police?" Tree continued. "I'm beginning to think you aren't."

Johnny Bravo allowed his eyes to go wide with surprise. "Melora? Not a Mountie? Don't tell me you've been lying, Melora."

"I don't want to talk about this," Melora said. "This is so ridiculous. I'm not going to be part of it."

"So, Tree." Johnny's eyebrows were lifted up in delight. "If she isn't who she says she is, who do you think she is?"

"Vic Trinchera's mistress, perhaps," Tree said.

Melora, red-faced, slapped Tree hard. His head jerked back, his ears ringing. Blood gushed from his nose. "You have no manners," she said.

"Take it easy, Melora," Johnny said. "He could have called you something much worse."

"I'm not that," she said in a hurt voice. "I'm not what he says I am."

Tree was holding his nose. Johnny Bravo tossed him one of the white linen napkins on the table. "Here you go, Tree. You're bleeding."

Tree took the napkin and looked at Shay. "And then there is Shay. The mystery woman. Partner of the late André Manteau? Muse? What were you to him? How do you play into this?"

"Tree has a point, Shay," Johnny said. "You're not exactly biker babe material. André usually liked them in denim with lots of tattoos."

Shay gave Johnny a cool, appraising look. "No tattoos, Johnny."

"And no André," Johnny shot back.

This isn't getting us anywhere,"she said.

Johnny met her gaze, unblinking. "It gets us to who you really are, Shay. And what it is you want."

"I want what the two of you want—what Callister here can help us with."

Nobody sitting at the table answered. The waiter, bug-eyed, arrived with the water. "Is anybody ready to order?" he said in a choked voice.

"Better give us a few more minutes, monsieur," Johnny Bravo said. "We've just started to beat one another up."

The waiter nodded and went away.

Tree, holding his nose, said, "You want the dog."

"The tie that binds," Johnny said. "The glue that sticks us together."

"Why your men came to my friend's boat last night," Tree said.

Johnny Bravo smiled when he said, "I don't know what you're talking about."

"Come on, Johnny. Don't be so shy about it. The Mexican wrestling masks were a nice touch."

Johnny looked surprised. "They showed up wearing masks?"

"Not that it was hard to figure out who they were."

Johnny shook his head. "I've got to get better help."

Shay looked sharply at Johnny. "I thought we had an agreement."

"We do," Johnny said.

"You weren't supposed to start with any of your nonsense. That was part of the agreement."

"I thought I might be able to move things along a little faster." He added with a shrug: "You can't blame a boy for trying."

Shay turned to Tree, training her direct, no-nonsense gaze on him. "What about it, Tree? What about the dog?"

"Supposing I have information that would help you locate what you're looking for?"

"See?" Johnny said excitedly. "Didn't I tell you?"

"He's got the dog," Melora agreed.

"What about it, Tree?" Shay, pressing.

The waiter was back, looking more gun-shy than ever.

"I want a club sandwich," Johnny Bravo said.

"Nothing for me," Shay said, thumping a forefinger against the menu for emphasis.

Melora let out a pained sigh.

Tree just shook his head, sending the dejected waiter away.

"Where were we?" Johnny Bravo said.

"The dog," Shay answered. She addressed Tree. "What do you want? Name a figure."

"Half a million dollars," Tree said promptly. "And an explanation."

To Tree's amazement, no one laughed and immediately dismissed such an outrageous demand. Instead, the three busied themselves trading glances. Finally, Shay said, "The money is fine. But at that price, you don't get an explanation."

"You mean you would pay half a million dollars for a dog, but you wouldn't tell me why?"

"Do you want the money or not?"

Tree hesitated before he said, "Yes, but I'll need some time."

Johnny's eyebrows once more rose toward his hairline. "Time? What do you need time for? You've got the dog. You know it. I know it."

"Thanks to you, Johnny, and your visit last night, in fact, I don't actually have the dog. I need forty-eight hours to get him back."

"Twenty-four," Melora said. "You got twenty-four hours. Then all bets are off."

"In the meantime, everyone stays away from me and my wife," Tree said. He had his eye on Johnny Bravo when he said this. "No more trashing houses. No more late-night visits."

Johnny Bravo said, "Perish the thought."

"Twenty-four hours," Shay reminded him. "You give up the dog in twenty-four hours."

35

Tree was no sooner back in the Hellcat than his cellphone sounded on the seat beside him.

"How are you doing?" Sonny Trinchera demanded.

"I'm doing fine, Sonny," Tree said. "How are you doing?"

"My brother's killer, did you find her?"

"It's being taken care of," Tree said.

"What's that mean?"

"It means this is nothing we should talk about over the phone," Tree said.

"Okay. Let's meet. I gotta get this settled."

"I need twenty-four hours," Tree said.

"Twenty-four hours? What do you need twenty-four hours for?"

"Do you want this settled or not?"

"Of course I do."

"Then I need some time to put a couple of things together. I'll be in touch as soon as I'm ready."

"Don't screw with me, Callister. I'm warning you, the Mortician isn't someone you mess around with. Understand me?"

"It's probably not a good idea to threaten me right now," Tree said.

"I'm not threatening," Sonny said. "I am making the situation clear to you."

"Twenty-four hours," Tree said.

Before Sonny could offer any more objections or threats, Tree ended the call.

Great, he thought. Now I'm in more trouble than ever.

As Tree looked out through the Hellcat's windshield, Shay Ostler, alone this time, carrying the Daft Punk helmet, swayed into the Biltmore's parking lot. Her lustrous hair floated around her as she moved. When she reached the Streetfighter, she pulled the helmet over her head, started the engine, and sped away. Tree turned into the street after her.

————————

Shay brought the Ducati Streetfighter to a stop outside an Art Deco house on a tree-lined street in South Beach.

Tree parked down the block, watching Shay get off her motorcycle and cross the street. As she approached the house, a figure stepped out. FBI Special Agent Max Hesselgesser embraced her. Shay kissed him hard on the mouth.

The two of them disappeared inside.

Tree pulled out his cellphone and used his forefinger to poke out a number.

Cee Jay Boone came on the line and said, "I hate it when you call me, Tree."

"Why is that?"

"Because you're going to take advantage of things that went on in the past, and ask me to do something I shouldn't be doing."

"This time it's different," Tree said. "I'm going to get you Edith Goldman's killer."

"I thought you didn't know anything about that," Cee Jay said.

"I didn't then. Now I do. Are you interested or not?"

"I'm interested if you have information that pertains to an ongoing police investigation," Cee Jay said in her formal detective voice. "But what I'm not interested in is sticking my neck out and helping you with things I shouldn't help you with."

"All I need is some information."

"What kind of information?"

"I need to know if there is an FBI agent attached to the Miami office by the name of Max Hesselgesser."

"Then what?"

"I also need information on a woman named Shay Ostler."

"I don't understand what I'm going to get out of this."

"I told you. Edith's killer."

"You seem pretty sure of yourself."

"I need to know about Hesselgesser and Ostler, and I need it in the next twenty-four hours," Tree said.

"This guy's name is Hesselgesser?"

"Max Hesselgesser," Tree said. "And Shay Ostler."

"How is she supposed to be connected to this?"

"She was working with André Manteau."

"The guy they found in your car."

"That's correct."

"Tree, what in God's name are you involved in?"

"That's what I need you to help me with," Tree said.

"I'll call you back," Cee Jay said, and hung up.

———————

Tree waited and watched as the street grew dark and the lights illuminated the trees lining either side of the roadway.

Cramped and tired, he fought to stay awake. Why did he do this? Madness. Evidence of a wasted detective life.

A single overhead light burned in the entranceway to Hesselgesser's apartment building, providing shadowy illumination for Shay's abrupt appearance. She stood on the front step struggling into the Daft Punk helmet before coming down along the walk to the Streetfighter. She sat astride the bike and started the engine. A couple of moments later, she was off down the darkened street.

He almost started after her, but then stayed where he was, wondering about Max Hesselgesser. Why hadn't he walked her out? He waited for a while and then, driven more by the cramp in his legs than anything, Tree got out and stretched against the side of the car. Blessed relief shot along his thigh. He opened the passenger door and reached into the glove compartment for the Glock.

Jamming it into his pocket, he hobbled across the street. He went up the steps. Green-painted iron bars blocked the way. There were bars in the arched windows flanking the entrance-way. A barred gate was ajar. He pushed it open and stepped into a tiled foyer decorated with big potted plants.

He crossed a tree-lined courtyard and went in another door opening into a kitchen. The kitchen led into a dining-living-room area. A guitar was propped against the wall. Tree went through the living room to the single bedroom.

Max Hesselgesser kneeled on the unmade bed. He was naked, wrists handcuffed behind his back. The top of his head had been blown off. Blood soaked the canary yellow bed sheets. Max's discarded clothing was strewn on the floor near the bed—evidence of his passion to get his pants off for Shay Ostler.

Tree thought about calling the police. He thought about all the ways that would complicate his life right now—the terrible delaying business involved in finding yet another body.

He didn't have time for that. Amazed to find himself thinking like this, he backed out of the bedroom and went out of the apartment.

The street was empty. He reached the Hellcat and got in and started the engine. As he drove off, he tried not to think of Max Hesselgesser hunched on a bed, his hands bound behind him, pieces of his head scattered across the room, victim of the beautiful, deadly Shay Ostler.

36

Tree called Rex on his cell on the way into Fort Myers. "Where are you?" Rex demanded.

"Sorry. I got delayed in Miami."

"I'm at a Kiwanis dinner, so I couldn't stick around. But Kelly's got the dog and is waiting for you at the office."

"Thanks, Rex."

"Just hurry up and get over there."

Kelly was waiting in Rex's office with Clinton when Tree finally reached the Chamber. Kelly wore a white blouse and pink shorts that set off the newly bronzed contours of her body. Island life was agreeing with her. She unhooked the leash so Clinton could jump up excitedly on Tree, who welcomed the attention and enthusiastically rubbed Clinton's ears.

"Thanks, sorry I'm late," Tree said.

"Hopefully, you were out there working on our story," Kelly said.

"Something like that."

"It wasn't so bad," Kelly said. "I'm not much of a dog person. But it's hard not to like this guy—particularly since he seems to be such an important part of our story."

Tree just looked at her.

"You'll notice I said *our* story," Kelly added.

"I noticed," Tree said.

"Tree, I don't like to sound desperate, but I do need this."

"I know that's what you're saying, Kelly. But I think you're confusing want with need."

"Please, Tree, don't make me say things I don't want to say." Kelly rose from the chair. "You and I have a deal, so let's both make sure we live up to it. I think we owe our past lives that much, don't you?"

"What does the past have to do with any of this?"

"You think it doesn't?"

"No."

"You owe me, Tree."

"For what? Kelly, you left me, remember?"

"I left you because you were a lousy husband who didn't give a damn about anything except his job and drinking with the guys."

Tree swallowed the bile he felt rising in his throat and said tightly, "You and I obviously have different perspectives."

"What are you saying? You weren't a lousy husband?"

Tree took a deep breath. "Okay, here's the thing. I need the next twenty-four hours to get this resolved."

Kelly nodded and said, "All right. I guess I don't have much choice, do I?"

She reached down and stroked Clinton's head. She seemed to be wrestling with what she was going to say next.

Tree said, "Okay, what am I missing?"

"Something I should tell you," she said. "Or maybe it's what I shouldn't tell you."

"What is it, Kelly?"

"It's Rex. He doesn't want me to say anything. He says it's no big deal."

"What's no big deal?"

"The surgery."

Tree felt his stomach drop. "What kind of surgery?"

"He's been complaining about being tired. He said he was feeling tightness in his chest. I went through the same thing with my second husband, so I pushed him into the car and drove him to his doctor. Turns out he needs a heart bypass. Sooner rather than later."

"Thanks for telling me, Kelly—and thanks for making him go to the doctor. He probably wouldn't have done it, if you weren't here."

"Now he's procrastinating about the surgery, and he shouldn't. The sooner they operate on him, obviously, the better."

"Should I talk to him?"

"He doesn't want you to know."

"Well, now I know," Tree said.

"He's not going to be very happy with me."

"Rex is like most men, willing to forgive you anything."

She tried on a wry smile. "Does that include you, Tree?"

"Hey, I was the lousy husband, remember?"

"Talk to him," Kelly said. "Maybe he'll listen to you."

37

What to tell Freddie when he arrived home? *Hi, honey. I found another dead body, but this time I didn't phone the police because it would disrupt the ridiculous plan I have hatched.* That story certainly would not fly. But in failing to tell it, Tree was once again lying by omission—a specialty of his, honed since becoming a private detective.

He and Freddie spent a several hours returning their disrupted house to some semblance of order, Clinton trailing around after them, endlessly curious about what they were up to, making sure he was never left alone. They were just thinking of turning in for the night when Cee Jay Boone called.

"Max Hesselgesser was assigned to the Miami office of the FBI. He's been there for the past six years. However, a couple of weeks ago, he retired," she said.

"So he's not an agent any longer," Tree said.

"No, and I gather he left under a cloud."

"What kind of cloud?"

"No one would talk over the phone, but something happened."

"What about Shay Ostler?"

"Nothing about her. Sure that's her real name?"

"I'm not sure of anything. Thanks, Cee Jay."

"Hold on. Tell me how Max Hesselgesser fits into Edith Goldman's murder."

"I'll know more about that tomorrow," Tree said.

"Don't jerk me around, Tree."

"I'll be in touch," Tree said.

Tree ended the call before turning to the unhappy Freddie. "What are you up to?" she demanded.

Tree gazed down at Clinton, who looked back, turning his head as though to ask, "What's up?"

"What about it, Clinton? What should I do next?"

"I should have known," Freddie said, sounding unhappier than ever.

Clinton padded over to Tree and leaned against his leg, lowering his head to make it easier for Tree to pet him. He made small sounds of contentment.

"Maybe we've been looking at this the wrong way," Tree said.

"What do you mean?"

"Something Crimson said to me. He said it wasn't the dog everyone was after."

"Then why is everyone after the dog?"

Tree undid Clinton's collar and held it up.

"What are you doing?" she asked.

"It's got to be the collar," Tree said.

"We've looked and looked at that fool collar," Freddie said. "How can we be missing anything?"

Instead of answering, Tree went into the garage, returning with a screwdriver.

"What are you doing?" Freddie asked.

Tree positioned the collar on the kitchen counter, and began to dig the flat edge of the screwdriver into one of the metal flowers. He finally pried one loose. It flipped away, revealing a hollow metal cylinder. There was nothing inside the hollow.

Tree did the same thing with a second flower and then a third. Three quarters of an hour later, he had pried off all the flowers, colored metal pieces littering the countertop. There was nothing inside any of the hollows.

"What did you think was going to be in there?" Freddie said.

"I don't know," Tree said. He looked at her and shrugged. "Diamonds," he said sheepishly.

"Diamonds? You thought the dog was carrying around a collar full of diamonds?"

"I may have been grasping at straws."

Clinton nuzzled his leg. Tree reattached the collar. Freddie got to her feet and yawned. "I'm going to bed," she announced. "Are you coming?"

"In a while."

"Tree, you're not going to solve this tonight."

"I know that, but tomorrow I'm going to have to either give up Clinton to three people who don't have his best interests at heart, or phone the police, who will take him away."

"I wish I could think of something, my love," Freddie said. "But right now I can hardly keep my eyes open." She came over and planted a kiss on his lips. "Don't stay up all night."

"No," he said distractedly.

Freddie slipped away. Tree drifted onto the terrace. Clinton followed and lay on his side beside Tree's chair, his shallow breathing the only sound in the night.

Tree sat thinking. But thinking about what? How stupid he was to leave Max Hesselgesser lying dead on a bed in Miami? How ill-equipped he was to deal with any of this? Yes, something like that. He forced himself to concentrate on Clinton. He reached down and petted Clinton's torso. The dog lifted his head appreciatively, stretched his long legs, and then lay still again.

"*It's not the dog they're after.*" The gospel according to the late Crimson.

Tree sat up.

If it wasn't the dog.

Maybe. Just maybe.

It was *where* the dog could take you.

38

"You sound like hell," Rex said when Tree phoned him.

"That's because I haven't slept," Tree said.

"At your age, you should be getting at least eight hours a night. Mind you, I'm not going to get that tonight. I've just finished with the Kiwanis dinner. Normally, I would drive myself home. But a certain so-called friend has stolen my Hellcat."

"Your so-called friend appreciates your sacrifice, Rex. Is Kelly picking you up?"

"She's on her way, so not to worry," Rex said. "What's up? Have you totaled my car?"

"Not yet," Tree said, "but I'm going to need it a little longer."

"Mind if I ask what's going on?"

"I was about to ask you the same question."

"You've been listening to Kelly, I suppose."

"She's worried about you. So am I."

"I'm okay."

"Are you?"

"I'm probably in better shape at the moment than you are."

"No argument there. But if you're supposed to have an operation, Rex, then you should have the operation."

"It's not an operation. That's old school. They call it a procedure."

"Okay. Have the procedure. After I'm gone, I need someone here to extol my virtues."

"It may take me a while to figure out exactly what those virtues are."

"You can do that while you're being operated on."

Rex said, "How did you and I ever become friends?"

"You took me in out of the rain, fed me, watered me, and raised me as your own."

"I didn't do much of a job."

"Which is why I need you to stick around. So you can continue to correct and improve my behavior."

For a time, neither man said anything. Then Tree said, "I love you, you old coot."

Rex said, "Don't call me an old coot."

———

Tree was approaching the outskirts of Miami, trying to keep his eyes open, when his cellphone sounded. He thought it was Freddie, but to his surprise it was Jim Devereaux calling from Montreal.

"Did I wake you up?" Devereaux asked.

"In fact, I'm driving to Miami," Tree said.

"At this time of night?"

"The Sanibel Sunset Detective Agency never sleeps."

"Look, it's probably nothing. But I've been working my contacts ever since we last talked."

"Much appreciated," Tree said.

"The name you gave me, Shay Ostler, it doesn't ring anyone's bell. But the fact she was hooked up with André Manteau, Le Manteau Noir—the Black Coat—leader of The Devil's Headsmen, a legend in Quebec biker circles, that got several people to thinking."

"Thinking about what?"

"Again, this is probably nothing. But there are stories about this teenager from Outremont, a very tony part of French-speaking Montreal, a stunner who hooked up with Manteau and the Devil's Headsmen, became one of them—someone willing to break an egg."

"Break an egg. I've heard that before."

"In the parlance of Montreal mobsters, you break an egg, you kill someone."

"This kid killed people?"

"She became a very good killer, apparently. A young woman who enjoyed her work. They called her La dame des trois, the Lady of the Three, because she liked to shoot her victims three times."

"Any idea what happened to her?"

"I'm not even sure if La dame des trois exists. Could be she's nothing more than an urban myth, la beauté qui est une bête—the beauty who's a beast."

"Except the beast killed someone tonight."

That gave Devereaux pause. "You know this for certain?"

"I'm afraid so," Tree said.

Devereaux issued a low whistle over the phone. "That might explain what happened to two of my favorite Montreal gangsters."

"Not to mention a lawyer and an FBI agent," Tree said. "But if she killed André Manteau, then who is she working for?"

"Maybe Johnny Bravo," Devereaux said. "He would certainly benefit from having Vic Trinchera out of the picture—and Manteau, too, for that matter."

Tree thought of Johnny at lunch with Shay Ostler and Melora Spark. None of it made much sense. All that drew everyone together was a dog named Clinton.

"What about a dog? Any of your underworld informants mention a dog?"

"You keep asking about this dog," Devereaux said, sounding confused. "I can't imagine how a dog fits into any of this."

"Yes, you're probably right," Tree said. "Thanks for your help, Jim."

"Keep in touch," Devereaux said. "I'm not sure what you're up to, but be careful."

Tree called Kelly Fleming. "You're on your way to pick up Rex?"

"Did you talk to him?" she asked.

"Just now," he said.

"And?"

"Don't hold me to this, but I believe in his irascible way he knows he has to do something, so he can stick around, and I can continue to make his life as difficult as possible."

"I hope he listens to you," she said.

"That story you're interested in," Tree said.

"Have you got something for me?" There was an undertone of tension in her voice.

"I might, but listen to me, Kelly, there is a certain amount of risk involved here."

"Oh, goody," she said.

"That you can't tell Rex about. At least not for now."

"Okay," Kelly said. "I won't say anything. Now what?"

"You have a camera?"

"I know where to get one," she said.

"Just you and a camera. No one else."

"Sure," Kelly said. "That's fine."

"Then here's what I need you to do."

39

Anastasia Avenue was quiet and empty, the houses lining either side of the street in darkness.

As soon as Tree got Clinton out of the car he was a dog transformed: panting excitedly, straining at his leash, and seeming to know exactly where he was headed—toward Vic Trinchera's elegant Mediterranean-style bungalow.

With Tree running to keep up, the dog veered up the drive onto a pathway running alongside the house.

Clinton came to a stop at the rear of a screened-in lanai. He raised a paw and started scratching at the screen door. Tree rattled the door and found it locked. He got his American Express card out of his wallet and slipped it between the doorframe and the latch. On cheaper storm doors usually the locking mechanism only held the latch in place. He wiggled the card around. To his surprise, the latch clicked and he was able to push the screen door open.

Curiously pleased with his successful attempt at breaking and entering—his dark, criminal side at work—he allowed Clinton to pull him across the lanai into the sitting room.

The dog made excited whimpering sounds. Tree had never seen him like this. "Easy boy," he said, "Take it easy."

He released Clinton from the leash. As soon as the dog was free, he charged out of sight down a hallway. Tree hurried after him into a master bedroom. Someone had gone through the drawers, pulling them out of the dresser occupying most of one wall, strewing their contents across the floor and the king-size bed.

Clinton, his tail slicing furiously back and forth, clawed at a closet door. Tree opened it up to reveal a rack of workout costumes in shades of navy blue and black. Vic had apparently decided to reduce his wardrobe to the essentials he found most comfortable. The track outfits formed a curtain behind which suitcases and nylon overnight bags were piled. Clinton pawed at the suitcases until Tree pulled them out of the closet. Now Clinton sniffed eagerly at something against the wall—the same brown and white kitty plush toy he had in his mouth when Tree met him. The kitten looked surprisingly lifelike, down on all fours with big, happy eyes. Tree picked it up and went into the bedroom where he placed it on the floor. Clinton swatted his paw at it, and immediately it sat up on its haunches and began waving its paws.

Clinton yelped, retreated a few feet, and then attacked the plush toy. This time the toy issued a meowing sound, and bounced back down on all fours. Clinton pounced, grabbing the toy in his mouth, shaking it vigorously—revenge for daring to wave its paws at him. And then with the toy firmly in his mouth, he bounded out of the bedroom.

Tree followed Clinton into the sitting room where he found him having the time of his life shaking his kitty nemesis around. Tree managed to pry the toy out of the dog's jaws. Clinton was not happy about this. He jumped up on Tree, demanding the return of his toy.

Tree turned it over in his hands. Its fake fur was slick from Clinton's drool. On the underside of the plush toy, a plastic trap door was visible. Tree snapped it open and found four double-A batteries inside. He removed the batteries.

That's when he saw the folded piece of paper. He removed the paper and opened it up. Someone had used a felt-tipped pen to scrawl words and numbers:

TODAY IS THE DAY

1225

368

Tree floated through the velvet night, Hank Williams singing on oldies radio. The silence of a falling star lighting up a purple sky. You got it, Hank, Tree thought. The saddest song ever written, a sad man listening, lost in the dark, his dog pressing his snout between the seats, in need of a reassuring pat. Hank Williams should have had a dog. But then, mused Tree, if he had a dog, he probably never would have written that saddest of all songs.

He stopped for gas at a Chevron station. He was dead tired as he punched in his debit card PIN number, waited until his purchase was approved, and then stuck the gas nozzle in the tank and began to fuel up, taking deep gulps of the early morning air to keep himself awake.

Clinton watched him through the rear windshield, the solemn expression that revealed nothing, yet said everything about unconditional love and the certainty that somehow Tree would keep him safe. Don't worry, my lovely dog, Tree thought, I'll keep you out of harm's way. If it's the last thing I do, I will do that.

I *am* so lonesome I could cry.

Suddenly, unaccountably, he found himself choked with emotion. A large woman in baggy shorts at the next pump gave him a strange look. He turned away quickly, taking in more air, ordering himself to pull it together. This was no time to start breaking down.

He finished filling the tank, returned the nozzle to the pump, and then leaned against the Hellcat punching out a number on his cellphone. It took only a couple of rings before Sonny Trinchera came on the line, sounding wide awake. "Yeah, what is it?"

"What are you doing up at this time of night?" Tree said.

"I never sleep," Sonny said. "That's how I keep ahead of everyone else. Tell me what you got."

"The results you're looking for," Tree said.

"What's that supposed to mean?"

"It means I've said as much as I'm going to say over the phone," Tree said. "I need to meet with you."

"When?" Sonny said. "Where?"

———————

Tree was turning onto Collins Avenue when he reached Johnny Bravo on his cellphone. He sounded wide awake, too. "Monsieur Detective," he said. "I was just thinking about you."

"Doesn't anyone sleep?" Tree said.

"I'll have plenty of time to sleep when I'm dead. Right now I am very much awake and thinking of you. Your twenty-four hours are just about up."

"I know that," Tree said. "It's why I'm calling—to set up a meeting."

Johnny paused before he said, "You'll be bringing the dog with you, of course."

"Put it this way," Tree said. "I will provide you with what you need."

"Yes? And what exactly is that?"

"What you don't need is the dog. You need what I'm going to give you."

Another pause before Johnny said, "And you've found it, is that what you're trying to say?"

"Something like that," Tree said.

"Then by all means, we must meet."

"I thought we should settle a couple of things first."

Johnny Bravo said, "What kind of things?"

"The price, for example. Now that I see what you're after, I believe my asking price is too low."

"There is no renegotiation. The price we agreed on is the price to be paid."

"Let's suppose at this meeting there's only the two of us. That could change the asking price, could it not?"

The pause this time was so long, Tree thought he might have lost the signal. But then Johnny Bravo said, "What have you in mind?"

40

The blocks of warehouses were ghostly shapes in the pre-dawn light. The Hellcat's headlights swept a massive mural featuring gray men in gray concrete cubicles topped with coils of barbed wire—the horror of life outside art.

Tree parked at the curb. He sat there for a few moments, gathering his thoughts. He breathed deeply four or five times and then opened the glove compartment and took out Rex's Glock 17. He shoved it into the waistband of his pants and got out of the car. He pulled Clinton out of the back.

Together, they made their way along the street to the converted garage formerly occupied by the late Crimson, aka André Manteau. He got out the notepaper he had found in the cavity of the kitty plush toy and keyed 1225 into the panel on the side of the sliding door. An electronic whir sounded, the garage door groaned at the thought of having to open at this time of the morning, but then it slowly lifted, exposing the dark interior.

Tree led Clinton inside, feeling his way uncertainly across the studio until he reached a wall and found a light switch. A patch of light flared, illuminating TODAY IS THE DAY in bold letters near a huge American flag. The flag hung over workbenches, trestle tables, and metal racks that housed the dozens of oils and collages Crimson churned out before his gangster past caught up with him.

Tree studied the other number printed on the notepaper: 368.

He went along the racks, inspecting the artworks they held. Each piece was numbered. In the second bin he looked through, he found 368, a small canvas, bubble-wrapped for protection, tucked between two of Crimson's massive collages. He pulled the canvas out and carried it over to one of the benches. He heard a sound and turned to see Melora Spark materialize out of the gloom. She was dressed in jeans and a V-necked T-shirt. Like so many of the people he had encountered lately, she pointed a gun at him.

"I don't suppose you have a gun, do you, Tree?"

"As a matter of fact, I do," Tree said.

"Then why don't you put that canvas down and take out your gun and slowly put it on the floor?"

Tree placed the canvas on the bench and then took out the gun and bent down to drop it to the concrete floor. Melora moved over and kicked the gun away. It skittered across the concrete. She kept her gun on Tree and glanced at the canvas.

She said, "So, you found it."

"Yes," Tree said.

"Vic was dumb about a lot of things," Melora said. "But he was a crafty old monster, I will give him that. He hid it in the last place anyone would think to look."

Clinton bared his teeth and uttered a low, threatening growl. Melora showed a flash of fear. "Keep that dog away from me or I'll shoot it."

"Don't," Tree said.

Clinton's head snapped forward accompanied by a loud bark. Melora responded by lifting the gun higher. "I'm warning you," she said.

"I've got the dog," Tree said. "He's not going to hurt you."

"I don't like dogs." Her voice rose and broke into ragged notes. "I will shoot that dog. I will."

She took a deep breath. Tree could see that she was on edge.

"Funny," Tree said. "All along I thought it was Clinton everyone was after. But really it was this painting. This is why you left the Mounted Police and why Max Hesselgesser retired early from the FBI. It's what brought Johnny Bravo to town, and it's what got at least three people killed."

Tree began to tear away at the bubble wrap.

"I don't think you should do that," she said, raising the gun higher.

But he didn't stop. Still holding Clinton, he managed to strip away the bubble wrap to reveal a somber oil of thatch-roofed cottages nestled among a copse of trees.

"A painting," Melora said.

"By Rembrandt," Tree said.

"So you do know," she said.

"A long time ago, Vic Trinchera stole it," Tree said.

Melora nodded. "Vic was a smalltime hood in Montreal in 1972. Then he decided to break into the Montreal Museum of Fine Art."

"Along with a couple of lowlife kids, André Manteau and Johnny Bravo," Tree said.

"Trouble was, they couldn't cash in their stolen property. It was too hot. Manteau and Johnny Bravo decided the robbery was a bust. But Vic knew he had something invaluable. All he needed was patience. He sat on the painting for years, brought it down to Florida when he moved here. When his world started to fall apart, everyone coming after him, what scared him the most was the thought of losing his Rembrandt."

Tree said, "Vic was sick, his rival, Johnny Bravo, was in town looking for him. He didn't want Johnny getting his hands on the painting. So, he decided to hide it in plain sight. Unbeknownst to anyone, he hid it here in the studio. He somehow got hold of the entry code and one night simply placed it among Crimson's works."

"Then Vic got himself killed."

"Yes, Shay Ostler acted a little too hastily when she pumped three bullets into him on Coral Way in Miami, after you left him."

Melora couldn't hide her surprise. "Shay?"

"She's a professional killer from Montreal. You didn't know that?"

"I knew she worked for André. I thought she wanted the painting like everyone else."

"Shay had other things in mind, including a contract to kill Crimson. She ended up killing Edith, too. I suppose Edith couldn't tell her what she wanted to know."

"But you were different, Melora. You were simply after the painting. And when Max found out about it, he wanted it, too, and that's how the two of you hooked up with Shay and Johnny Bravo. Trouble was, you couldn't find the painting."

"I did have one clue. The dog. That awful dog." Her voice broke again. She tightened her grip on the gun. "Vic always said the dog knew everything. I thought he was joking. But it turns out he wasn't joking at all."

"However, when you came looking for Clinton, he had disappeared."

"I knew that Vic had been in touch with you, and you were at his house when I picked him up. As unlikely as it seemed, maybe you had the dog."

"All the information anyone needed to find the painting Vic hid in Clinton's favorite toy."

"I wonder why he did that."

"Maybe he was hoping someone like me would find the painting, and someone like you wouldn't."

"And you figured it out, Tree. I'm impressed. Until you met us at the hotel, I wouldn't have thought you could figure out much of anything."

Tree held the painting up. "Here it is, Melora. The stuff dreams are made of."

Melora frowned. "What are you talking about?"

"Never mind," Tree said. "I watch too many old movies."

Holding the painting, Tree wasn't prepared for Clinton's sudden lunge. The leash snapped out of his hand. Freed of any restraint, Clinton dashed forward, barking and snarling at the startled Melora.

"Stop that dog," she cried. "Stop him!"

Tree put the canvas back on the table and started after Clinton. "It's all right, he's not going to hurt you."

"Get him away from me. Get him away!"

Clinton's teeth bared in an ugly snarl. His barks had descended into a low, unsettling growl. Head lowered, he came at Melora.

"Keep away!" She was screaming now and her face had gone white. Tree frantically called to Clinton, but he kept closing in on Melora—the hunter stalking his prey.

Melora cried out and the gun rose in a black blur in her moving hand.

"*No!*" Tree's turn for the panicky scream.

Without thinking, he blindly threw himself at her. The gun went off. Melora continued screaming. Somehow Tree got his hand on Melora's wrist. But she was a whole lot stronger than he imagined. He knocked her back against one of the trestle tables and for a moment the two grappled together for the gun. Then, with a further burst of unexpected strength, she broke free.

Four men loomed in the cavity of the garage, spreading out against the uncertain light. Three of the men wore Mexican wrestling masks. But not Johnny Bravo, a pale wraith with a gun in his hand. "I'll take the painting," he said with a certainty that, under the circumstances, Tree would not have thought was warranted.

"No, you don't," Melora said with equal certainty.

That's when Johnny shot her, a deafening hollow bang in the garage interior that made Tree jump and Clinton yelp in alarm.

Melora staggered back, a bloody hole where her left eye had been a moment before. Johnny walked over to the painting. The tallest of the three men with him said in a raspy voice, "Sorry, Johnny."

And then he shot Johnny Bravo in the chest. Johnny managed to get a shot off, and that induced more gunshots from the other masked men.

Tree, ducking down, got hold of Clinton's trailing leash, and yanked him back. He crawled around a table, hugging the dog to him. More gunfire sounded. Bullets ricocheted around. Tree saw the Glock lying on the floor. He reached over and grabbed it. He saw Raspy-voice Guy, the Rembrandt under his arm, disappear out the door.

Abruptly, the gunfire stopped. Johnny Bravo's voice broke the silence: "Tree, you don't have a gun, do you?"

"I'm afraid I do, Johnny," Tree called back.

"Well, those bastards shot me."

"Your own people," Tree called back.

"Crazy, huh? Shows you can't trust anyone."

"Are they still out there, Johnny?"

"Doesn't look like it, Tree. Looks like they ran away."

"How badly are you hurt?"

"It's bad," Johnny Bravo said. "I'm bleeding like a stuck pig, so you might as well give me the painting."

"I'm sorry you're shot, Johnny, but I don't have the painting."

"I guess they took it with them. Doesn't that beat all? I really am bleeding, Tree. I'm going to have to get to a hospital."

"Let me call an ambulance."

"Sure, Tree, call an ambulance." Johnny's voice sounded weak. "I'm coming over there to get that painting in the meantime."

"It's like I told you, Johnny. I don't have it." Clinton trembled against Tree, his whole body shaking.

"That's right, Tree," Johnny Bravo said. "That's what you told me."

"I'm going to call an ambulance, Johnny. But I don't want you to shoot me, okay?"

Johnny didn't respond. Tree peered around the edge of the table. He couldn't see anything.

"Johnny," Tree called. But there was no answer.

From outside the garage, Tree heard the high-pitched scream of sirens, growing steadily louder. "The cavalry is on its way, Johnny. You don't want them to find you here, that's the last thing you want."

Still no response from Johnny. The wail of the sirens grew to a crescendo and then abruptly stopped. If the police were on their way, they were not, for the moment at least, on their way to Crimson's studio. He ventured a glance above the trestle table.

The garage was empty, except for Melora, who lay face down on the concrete floor and Johnny Bravo on his back, blood pouring from his chest. Neither of them was moving.

Tree called to Clinton and the dog struggled to his feet, looking up at Tree with imploring eyes, as though apologizing for moving so slowly.

"Are you all right, baby boy?" Tree said. "What's the matter?"

Clinton responded by lying down again. Tree feared the dog had been hit by a bullet. But there was no sign of a wound. "Clinton, we have to go. Come on, boy. Get up."

But Clinton just looked up at him, beseeching. Finally, Tree had no choice but to bend down and with difficulty lift the dog up in his arms. Clinton struggled a bit, not liking this. But he quickly exhausted himself and settled so that Tree could carry him out into the street. He went around the corner to where the Hellcat was parked. He managed to get the rear door open and then place Clinton on the back seat. Clinton lay there, panting hard, anxious.

"It's going to be all right, boy," Tree said in a gentle voice. "It's going to fine. I'm going to get you help."

Tree got behind the wheel and started the engine. Well, he thought as he drove off down the street, this was interesting.

When it came to a choice between a dog and a Rembrandt painting—he had chosen the dog. Now that must say something about him.

Except he couldn't decide what that was.

41

Driving the Hellcat out of Miami, Tree expected police to come after him. "There are two bodies lying in a Wynwood garage," he imagined them saying once they surrounded him. "We think you're behind this. You caused all this mayhem, you and that dog."

But there were no police in the gray morning. By the time he reached Fort Myers, the sun had broken through and risen high and bright in a clearing sky. Another perfect Florida day. No murder on a day like this. That was all far behind him in dangerous Miami; here in peaceful Fort Myers murder was an impossibility.

The parking lot at the Tôt Funeral Home was nearly full. Tree managed to find a shady spot so he could leave Clinton in the car. He reached into the glove compartment and took out the Glock pistol.

As he approached the front entrance to the funeral home, the door opened. Raspy-voice Guy stepped back to allow Tree admittance. He took note of the Glock in Tree's hand. "Hey there, Mr. Callister," he said. "No need for that." Raspy-voice Guy looked freshly pressed in a dark suit that barely contained his body.

"Glad to hear it," Tree said.

Inside, Balding Guy, also in a dark suit, positioned himself near one of the potted plants. Pockmarked Guy nodded from his place near partially open double doors.

"Tree said, "I like you boys better when you're wearing your Mexican wrestling masks."

"Tree's got a gun," said Raspy-voice Guy casually, as if everyone who came into the funeral home brought a gun along.

"I keep telling you, the man's a comedian," said Balding Guy.

Through the opening Tree could see a memorial service in progress. A disembodied voice remembered "Jim's Georgia boyhood …"

The voice drifted off. Tree focused on Sonny Trinchera tucked into one of the easy chairs positioned around the foyer to catch grieving relatives too weak with grief to reach the exit. One of those relatives occupied a chair at the end of the room. Draped in black, she sat with her back to them, her head obscured by a wide-brimmed black hat.

"You're late," Sonny said. He did not get out of the chair. "What are you doing with a gun?"

"Just in case you have any ideas about shooting me," Tree said.

"Why would I shoot you?"

"I don't know, Sonny. Why would you?"

"You caught me just in time. I'm on my way back to Montreal for my brother's funeral."

"A time of great mourning and sadness, I'm sure," Tree said.

"So is everything taken care of?"

"Melora is dead if that's what you mean."

"You killed her?"

Tree shook his head. "Johnny Bravo took care of that."

"Where's Johnny now?"

"Let's stop the charade. I'm sure your boys here have already filled you in on what happened."

"Serves the bastard right," Sonny said. "Although I kind of liked Johnny."

"Now you can go back to Montreal, bury your brother, and run it all, just like you always planned," Tree said. "You even got the painting everyone wanted."

"What do I care about a painting?" Sonny's face had gone blank. "And what's this you're talking about? Run everything? What kind of nonsense is that?"

"You killed your brother, Sonny."

"My brother was a jerk," Sonny said. "He wouldn't listen to me. I tried talking to him. For years I tried. But he would never listen."

"So you had Shay kill him."

"Who's that? I don't know who you're talking about."

"She's the professional killer who works for you."

Sonny cracked a mirthless smile. "You've been watching too many gangster movies. I'm a businessman. I don't have anything to do with killers."

"What I still can't figure out is why you hired me."

"Like I told you. Find my brother's killer. Melora Spark. You did a good job. Congratulations. You're a great detective."

"Come on, Sonny. It's just the two of us. No one's going to believe me, even if I do tell the police—and I'm not going to tell them anything, provided I get what I want from you."

Sonny measured him for a couple of beats, the way he might have studied a corpse in a coffin.

"Okay. Fair enough. I'm willing to pay you for your work. How much do you want?"

Tree shook his head. "Better hold onto your money. You're probably going to need it."

"You don't want the money?" Tree had finally induced a look of surprise on that horse-face. "What's wrong with you?"

"That's a good question," Tree said.

"I don't get it. If you don't want money, what do you want?"

"A dog," Tree said.

Tree checked on Clinton in the car and then waited until the woman in the wide-brimmed hat came out. She removed the hat and Tree thought how lovely Kelly Fleming looked in black. It was her color. He wondered if she would wear black to his funeral. He wondered whether she would even attend his funeral.

He said, "Are you okay?"

"I've never been so scared in all my life," she said. "My idea of news is interviewing kids at a petting zoo."

"Did you get it?"

She gave a tense smile and held up the compact Canon HD camcorder, and then slipped it into her shoulder bag. "Not that I understood everything," she said. "Those guys in there are so creepy-looking."

"You wanted a story, this is the story," Tree said.

"Yes, but where is the Chicago angle?"

"I guess I am the Chicago angle. Did you take a cab here?"

"Just like you told me," she said.

"Good, I'll drive you back. Get in."

Kelly opened the passenger door and saw Clinton. "I don't think this dog is doing very well," she said.

He looked back at Clinton, and felt his stomach tighten. "It's all right, boy. It's going to be all right."

Kelly said, "I think you'd better have a vet take a look at him."

42

A story about a dog, a gangster, and an invaluable lost Rembrandt." Kelly's eyes gleamed with excitement. "This isn't local, Tree. This is network. This is Scott Pelley and *Sixty Minutes.*"

"As long as you make sure the police get a copy of the video you just recorded."

"I can't believe you pulled this off," Kelly said. "I didn't think you had it in you."

"All I'm concerned about is the dog," Tree said. "That's the only reason I did any of this—for Clinton."

"All this for a dog," Kelly said. "Who would believe it?"

Anyone who ever owned a dog, Tree thought. They would believe.

———————

Tree dropped Kelly off at the Chamber of Commerce Visitors Center, amid promises to get the video and the story to CBS as well as to Sanibel Police Detective Cee Jay Boone.

As he drove, Tree reassured Clinton it was going to be okay.

And it was. It was going to be okay.

Not to worry.

At Dayton's, he found Freddie in the midst of a meeting. The fleeting relief on her face disappeared as soon as she saw his grim expression. She told the others they would have to continue this later.

"Are you all right?"

"No," he said. The word choked in his throat.

"What do you need, my love?" Gentle words from wonderful Freddie—the words that just might get him through.

She followed him out to the parking lot. When she saw Clinton, her eyes welled with tears. Then she caught herself, took a deep breath, and got into the back with him. Clinton managed to lift his head so he could lay his snout on Freddie's lap.

Tree started up again. He could hear Freddie on the phone, calling a veterinarian she knew. Her voice was calm. They had to see him right away. Tree tamped down his rising sense of panic, forced himself to concentrate on the road.

It was going to be all right, he said to himself for the umpteenth time.

But then it wasn't all right at all.

Suddenly, the rear window shattered, sending a spray of glass through the interior. Clinton yelped in alarm. Freddie cried out as Tree hit the brakes and fought to keep the Hellcat on the road. Another bullet thumped into the side of the car. Tree, fighting with the wheel, glanced in his rearview mirror and saw the black and yellow of the Ducati Streetfighter. Shay performing one last hit before departing South Florida. Apparently, Sonny Trinchera had no faith in the promise of Tree's silence.

Shay swung her bike into the passing lane so that it came abreast of the Hellcat. Shay twisted to face him, a black robot with a gun. Tree took his foot abruptly off the gas pedal and the Streetfighter sped past. Shay swerved the bike back into Tree's lane, ahead of him now. Tree hit the gas, speeding up, intending to run into her. But Shay, realizing what Tree was trying to do, rocketed ahead. Freddie called out: "Tree, what's happening?"

"Hang on!" was all he had time for. There was too much traffic in the other direction so that he couldn't pass. From behind him, he heard an impatient horn.

A break in the oncoming traffic and Tree stomped on the gas. Once again the Hellcat lived up to its name, as it sprang into warp speed, no valet mode on this baby, seven hundred race horses, the Hellcat unleashed. It flew abreast of the Streetfighter. But then—and not even Hellcat horses could defeat this—an oncoming car and looming head-on disaster. Tree hit the gas and turned the wheel, thrusting the Hellcat smartly back into the right lane, a hair before the oncoming car flew past, angry horn at full blast. But now, the Hellcat once again was in the wrong place—fronting the Streetfighter.

And Shay had him in her sights.

Tree glanced at the speedometer. The Hellcat galloped comfortably along at over one hundred miles per hour, Periwinkle Way a passing blur. Despite the speed, a glance in the rearview mirror showed Shay in ominously close pursuit—the Streetfighter living up to its name.

The traffic cop at the corner of Periwinkle and Causeway Road jumped away in alarm as Tree braked, throwing up dust into the intersection, a breathtaking left turn—a turn he could not have ever previously imagined.

He hoped against hope that Shay would not be able to match that turn, but as he headed onto the causeway off the island, there was the Streetfighter, veering into the passing lane.

Tree caught another glimpse of the helmeted Shay, taking her time, aiming the gun. Abruptly a rusting pickup with what looked like a refrigerator strapped to its metal bed, materialized, as though the gods had thrown this groaning impediment in front of him to challenge the mighty Hellcat. He slammed the brakes, the Hellcat fishtailing wildly to show its disdain for such an unexpected maneuver. With Shay crowding him on the left, there was no way of escape. Imagining Shay beginning to squeeze the trigger, he could only cry out, "Freddie!"

Then, just as suddenly as she was there, Shay was gone in an explosion of metal as a big garbage truck, headed onto the island, smashed into the Streetfighter. In his sideview mirror,

Tree could see the motorcycle lift into the air, so much twisted, gleaming yellow and black carbon fiber against the stark blue of the sky—and Shay, a black-clad rag doll still attached to her machine as it sailed in slow motion over the protective bridge railing.

"What was that?" Freddie, breathless in the back.

"It's all right," Tree said, slowing. "Everything is okay."

"Quit saying that," Freddie snapped, an uncharacteristic show of frustration and anger. "Because it's not."

He said, "Just hold on. We're almost there."

Not very reassuring, but closer to the truth.

43

Somehow, they were in the parking lot at the Bob Riggs Veterinary Clinic. Tree carefully lifted Clinton out, holding him in his arms, a limp, heaving body, completely, utterly trusting in his arms.

Tree murmured something to him, words, more reassurances, following Freddie into a reception area that featured paintings of cute dogs and cats. Two anxious-looking young women in green hospital smocks were ready to usher them along a hallway and into a tiny room containing a medicine cabinet and a stainless steel table.

"I need a blanket for him, something," Tree said in a strained voice. "I can't put him down on that metal."

One of the women rushed away and returned with a padded blanket that she placed on the table. Tree lowered Clinton onto it. The dog looked up at him with pleading eyes. Freddie was right there, stroking Clinton's coat.

Bob Riggs entered, iron gray hair, tanned face, the picture of the middle-age runner in perfect health. "Okay, let's see what we have here," Riggs said.

A stethoscope was brought into play, along with gentle prodding. Yes, Tree thought. A doctor with a stethoscope. A professional who knew what he was doing. Clinton was in good hands. He was going to be okay. Tree was certain of that.

Riggs stopped and looked up at Freddie and Tree, his features glum. Tree felt his stomach drop. Cold fear rose in him.

"I would have to do tests to be certain, but it looks like he's suffered a stroke," Riggs said.

"What does that mean?"

"I'm afraid there's not a whole lot I can do for him," Bob Riggs said.

"There must be something," Tree said. The words sounded hollow and clichéd.

Riggs looked helplessly at Tree. "Letting him go. That's probably the biggest favor we could do for him at this point."

"Just like that?" The anguish caused his voice to break.

"I don't know what else to tell you," Riggs said.

Freddie held Clinton close and said, "He's in pain, Tree. I can feel his whole body trembling."

The tears streamed down Tree's face. "I told him everything was going to be all right. I told him that. I promised him I would keep him safe—that I would protect him."

"You've done that, my love," Freddie said. "You've done all that and more."

"So, now I kill him? After all we've been through, I kill him?"

"You don't kill him," Freddie said quietly. "You help him."

She nodded at the doctor. He left the room. Tree took Freddie's hand. "I can't believe this," Tree said.

"I know, darling, I know."

Riggs returned with a syringe. Tree and Freddie held Clinton and took turns stroking his head. They told him how much they loved him. They told him again and again.

Riggs leaned over Clinton. He slipped the needle into the dog's side.

When the final moment came, Clinton lifted up his fine head as if hearing something far away. Tree was certain he could see Clinton's spirit rise out of him. Then Clinton's body relaxed and his head dropped to the table. His eyes became lifeless.

And he was gone.

Freddie wrapped herself around Tree as they approached the car. "There are bullet holes in the Hellcat," he said. "Rex is going to kill me."

"Rex will understand," Freddie said.

"Not when I tell him the rear windshield is also missing."

The causeway was closed. They heard the news on the Hellcat's radio as they sat in the vet's parking lot. A terrible accident involving a motorcycle and a garbage truck. The truck driver was okay, but the female driver of the bike was reported dead. The name of the deceased had not been released by Sanibel Island police.

Tree turned off the engine and said he was in no shape to drive, anyway. They got out of the vehicle. Tree studied a huge dent in the side of the Hellcat. Where did that come from, he dimly wondered.

There was a park bench not far away. Freddie and Tree sat together and held hands and wept. Tree could not remember crying so hard. He was amazed by the depth of his grief. Freddie, as usual, was the stronger of the two; this was life, things happen. They had done their best. At least Clinton was with the people who loved him at the end. Think of that.

That only brought more tears. What a blubbering fool he was. Gangsters, crooked cops, female assassins, corpses—they all defeated him, left him feeling alone at the edge of a darkening world.

"There is light," Freddie said, holding his hand tight in hers. "We're the light, the two of us; what we have—the getting through bad stuff like Clinton's death together."

"I know," Tree said. "But right now I feel like I'm on a road lined with tombstones."

She reached out and took his hand and said nothing.

"What's more," Tree continued, "I'm afraid that when you hear the whole story of what happened you'll be so angry you're going to be finished with me."

"My love," she said, "I may get angry with you. But I am never finished with you."

"There's going to be a mess to deal with."

"That's okay. We'll deal with it together. We stick together. We see it through—that's our deal, and nothing breaks that deal."

She stood and held her hand out to him. "Come on, Tree," she said. "Let's go home."

He took her hand and stood. "Yes," he said. "Let's do that. Let's go home."

Afterword: The Real Clinton

Writing *The Hound of the Sanibel Sunset Detective* was an experience filled with joy and sadness. On the one hand, the novel allowed me to bring back to life Clinton, the beloved family member we lost at the age of fourteen in July 2013. To have him running happily on the beaches of Sanibel and Captiva Islands, loved and loving again, was an unexpected delight.

On the other hand, I was reminded constantly that this was only a story, that Clinton really was gone and even the most artfully fashioned words could never really bring him back. In the past five years, I have lost my mother and several of my dearest friends, people who were close and played an extraordinary role in my life.

But I must say, the loss of Clinton, our French hound, hit me harder than the loss of just about anyone else. He was my baby boy, the friend I had with me day in and day out, the one certainty in an uncertain life, always welcoming at the door with a shoe in his mouth, his recurring present for returning friends.

As he does for Tree and Freddie, Clinton brought us untold amounts of joy while he was alive. I have said many times that my wife, Kathy, and I would not have had a social life in Toronto, Montreal, or Milton, Ontario, without Clinton. Thanks to him, we met people and made friends who are still in our lives.

Clinton even slept with us. Try as we might to be firm, and not have him on the bed, we soon gave up trying to resist the irresistible. I don't believe he ever recovered from his inability as he grew old to climb the stairs and be with us. The last year of his life, I never slept through the night, slipping constantly downstairs to console an upset dog who only wanted to be with his pals.

The novel, like the other four in the series, is intended as an entertainment, and hopefully you, the reader, have not been disappointed.

However, writing the book also gave me the opportunity to explore within a fictional framework this deep, passionate love affair we have for our pets, how they manage to work their way into our lives and our hearts in ways we never could have imagined.

Any suggestion that they do not become family members is, of course, ludicrous. Only people who have not experienced pets would argue differently. Not only are they members of the family, they manage to become the most important members. We used to say, only half-jokingly, that Clinton didn't live with us, we lived with Clinton.

The looming tragedy of all this, the cosmic joke the gods have chosen to play, is that our beloved pets do not stay long. We love and protect them in life, but then, all too soon, we must orchestrate their deaths. It is the heartbreak of our pet love—they must exit long before we do, leaving us shattered.

Kathy and I go on, we muddle through. But it's not the same without Clinton. There remains an emptiness in the house every time we enter, and I doubt that will change any time soon. The memory of Clinton lingers always, the wonderful times we had with him, the ways in which he enriched our lives. Why, he even helped me write a book.

My unforgettable boy.

Acknowledgments

The usual suspects saved me repeatedly from myself: Kathy Lenhoff, first reader and incredible wife; David Kendall and Ray Bennett, longtime friends and hardnosed editors; Ric Base, brother extraordinaire, without whom these books would not be possible.

We introduce a couple of new members to the editorial team with this book. Susan Holly not only runs MacIntosh Books, one of the great independent bookstores on Sanibel Island, but is also a meticulous editor. Thanks to Susie and her eagle eyes, *The Hound of the Sanibel Sunset Detective* is a whole lot better than it would otherwise have been.

Ann Kornuta, a talented Milton, Ontario, artist, previously created the map of Sanibel-Captiva for the books. This time I asked her to bring Clinton to life for the cover. She's done an extraordinary job capturing that mixture of the comic and the elegant that was so much a part of his personality.

Over the course of writing five books, I have shamelessly exploited family members and have not hesitated to do so again. Thanks to my son, Joel, enthusiastic reader, and daughter, Erin, whose own efforts to write a novel help to improve mine.

Many thanks to my nephew, Eric Base, and his partner, Lorena Inostroza, for introducing me to the delights and mysteries of Miami. Alicia Base is the world's best sister-in-law, maintaining remarkable patience and good humor over the years in the face of repeated visits from a certain freeloading brother-in-law.

Finally, a word about Kim Hunter, aka The Driver. As regular readers know, such is my international renown that Kim drives me to Florida each November in his pickup truck. He still does not seem to understand that he must show more respect to a famous author, but I thank him, anyway.

The Sanibel Sunset Detective

Everyone on Sanibel Island, Florida, thinks former newspaperman Tree Callister is crazy to become a private detective. The only client he can attract is a twelve-year-old boy who has seven dollars with which to hire Tree to find his mother.

The Sanibel Sunset Detective Returns

The beautiful wife of a disgraced media mogul is certain her husband is having an affair. She hires Tree Callister to get the evidence. Then the mogul turns up dead on Sanibel Island, and not only is Tree's client arrested, but he finds himself accused of being an accessory to murder.

Another Sanibel Sunset Detective

Private Detective Tree Callister's marriage is in jeopardy, his son is in trouble, a guy with a machete threatens to cut off his hands, and a mysterious woman can't decide whether she wants to kill him—or seduce him.

The Two Sanibel Sunset Detectives

Madi and Josh are smart kids. Except they don't know what their father does for a living. That's where Private Detective Tree Callister comes in. Tree sets out to find the truth only to encounter vengeful cops and a murderous female drug lord who decides that Tree is her next victim.

Coming Soon

The Four Wives of the Sanibel Sunset Detective

Tree Callister is blissfully married to his wife, Freddie Stayner. However, there are three former wives with whom he must deal. They have gathered on Sanibel Island where Tree is supposedly happily retired from being the island's only private detective. All three wives are in trouble, and they expect Tree to get them out of it. The ensuing complications include fraud and murder—not to mention an increasingly unhappy fourth wife.

Contact Ron

ronbase.com
ronbase.wordpress.com
ronbase@ronbasc.com

CPSIA information can be obtained at www.ICGtesting.com
Printed in the USA
LVOW12s1117241014

410320LV00002B/2/P